Praise for Shannon Stacey's
No Surrender

"Spanning the globe from an icy cold winter in Canada to the sultry heat in South Africa, and with an amazing cast of intriguing characters, both good and bad, NO SURRENDER kept me on the edge of my seat for the whole ride."

~ *Romance Junkies*

"No Surrender is an instant favorite with its elements of danger, suspense, outstanding teamwork and most importantly, the love you can't miss."

~ *Joyfully Reviewed*

"Once again, Stacey keeps the reader on the edge of their seat, on a roller coaster of an adventure."

~ *I Just Finished Reading*

D1601269

Look for these titles by
Shannon Stacey

No Surrender

Shannon Stacey

A SAMHAIN PUBLISHING, LTD. publication.

Samhain Publishing, Ltd.
577 Mulberry Street, Suite 1520
Macon, GA 31201
www.samhainpublishing.com

No Surrender
Copyright © 2010 by Shannon Stacey
Print ISBN: 978-1-60504-743-0
Digital ISBN: 978-1-60504-724-9

Editing by Angela James
Cover by Scott Carpenter

First Samhain Publishing, Ltd. electronic publication: August 2009
First Samhain Publishing, Ltd. print publication: June 2010

Dedication

For my three guys, who spent countless hours brainstorming and problem solving with me. Not only did your interest and support warm my heart, but you made the process a joy. I'm sorry I couldn't use the Basque Separatists. Maybe next time.

Chapter One

"Heat signature, two o'clock, six meters." Gallagher watched the muted green blob move through the floor plan superimposed on his screen like a radioactive Pac-Man.

Carmen Olivera tapped twice on her microphone to confirm.

On another screen he watched some gaudy décor flash by through the small camera lens Carmen wore. Because the home they were rummaging through belonged to a Canadian billionaire, he'd expected some antiques and shit, but so far he hadn't seen anything that didn't remind him of his little sister's Barbie dream house.

He also hadn't seen what they'd come looking for. Jean Arceneau was suspected of laundering money and performing other unsavory favors for a particularly nasty terrorist regime, but the Feds couldn't prove it.

Arceneau had not only some serious cash flow, but heavy political clout, making his own government reluctant to expose the man to a potentially embarrassing investigation. That reluctance held other interested governments at bay.

So the Devlin Group had been called in because things like jurisdiction, warrants and probable cause didn't mean jack to them. The boss, Alex Rossi, had sent the pair to Canada to engage in some serious snooping. Carmen's job was to find evidence Arceneau was involved with the terrorists. Gallagher's job was to make sure nobody killed her while she snooped.

"If there was nothing in the office, there's probably nothing to find," Carmen said in a barely-there voice. "But I'll check the bedrooms to be sure."

Ten minutes later, the master bedroom had yielded nothing, but several four-wheel drive complications were approaching at a noticeably high rate of speed from the west. From his vantage point on the roof, Gallagher watched the Escalades getting bigger in his binoculars.

"Incoming, Carmen," Gallagher said. "Arceneau, probably, and I'm guessing some goons."

"He's supposed to be in the city."

"He didn't get the memo. And they're moving fast."

"Just let me check the kid's room. It'll be clean, but at least I'll have looked everywhere."

After three hours of maneuvering Carmen through the multimillion-dollar *camp*, keeping her one step ahead of housekeeping and security staff from his less than comfortable seat against a chimney, Gallagher was ready to blow that popcorn stand.

"E.T.A. less than two minutes."

"On my way out now."

"It's all clear to the rear library window." It was the way she'd gone in, and the staff was mostly in the kitchen area, so Gallagher started packing his gear, except for the comm piece over his ear.

The vehicles were turning onto the main loop of the driveway in front of the house when it all started going to shit.

"I'm going back for a sec," Carmen said.

"Negative. Subject entering residence in less than one

minute."

"It'll take me thirty seconds, tops."

Shit. Gallagher popped the thermal imaging screen out of his bag again. Carmen was retracing her steps to Isabelle Arceneau's room.

"Carmen, the girl's what...early twenties? She's not involved. Intel isn't even sure she's ever spent a night in that room."

"Even fishier. Have you ever met a college girl who leaves her pretty pink diary on her desk for anybody to read?"

Carmen didn't know it, but Gallagher had a teenaged sister, and there was no way in hell she'd leave her diary out in the open. That didn't mean, however, a daughter wasn't devious enough to have a fluff-filled, good-girl journal for Daddy to find and keep a real one well-hidden.

"Our objective is evidence against Arceneau, not Orlando Bloom fantasies," he reminded her.

The comm was silent long enough for the Escalades to slide to a stop in front of the house. Men spilled out of the vehicles with guns drawn—a *lot* of guns. Their ill-timed return was definitely no accident.

As they charged the house, they left Gallagher's line of sight. "Go. *Now.*"

"Holy shit, Gallagher. This diary—"

"You tripped something, Carm. Something that called in Arceneau without alerting the staff. You need to get the fuck out of there." He kept his eyes on his screen, waiting for her retreat.

"This is what we came for. A list of every transaction he's made and details of—"

"*Move*, Carmen!" Red blobs were dispersing across the

ground floor with alarming speed. "Downstairs is blocked. Plan B."

Since they didn't exactly *have* a Plan B, Gallagher shoved everything but his comm and his Glock 19 into his pack and strapped it on.

"Yeah, Plan B." She actually laughed. "Meet you at the bird in twenty."

And *shit* again. It had taken them forty to hike in, and he wasn't letting her cover that much ground alone. "I'll cover you from here."

"I'm not having that discussion again. Bird in twenty."

Gallagher argued with himself all the way down the side of the house.

The Devlin Group's NY office was probably still ringing with the echoes of their last *discussion.*

When an explosion had rocked the DG headquarters and put him at the reins of a hunt for a rogue agent, he'd sidelined Carmen into a non-active role. He'd whistled a bullshit tune about her having done a job with the guy and keeping the mission to a few non-conflicted personnel, but she hadn't danced. And she could seriously hold a grudge.

And there was no way in hell he could tell Carmen the real reason he'd pushed her outside the circle. Gallagher had feared the operation would get particularly messy and—with him stuck in an administrative role—didn't want her out there in it.

As a qualified, seasoned agent, Carmen would have blown her lid at such an overprotective measure, and rightly so. What he didn't know was how she'd react to learning his need to keep her safe was a lot more personal.

Gallagher made the tree line without being spotted, building and discarding scenarios in his head.

He could go back in after her, guns blazing, but if they lived, she'd kill him after. There was also the matter of being seriously outnumbered. He could create a distraction—make them believe he'd triggered the alarm and was out of the house. Carmen could sneak out while they were shooting at him. Major drawbacks, besides the part where he got shot at—he'd gone in the direction of the chopper and she'd still be pissed.

Or he could do as he was told and head for the helicopter. Being invisible was her specialty, after all.

But, dammit, he *knew* they hadn't tripped any alarms. Even though logic pointed to that, his gut told him it wasn't anything they'd done in the house. Something else was going on.

Carmen tapped three times on her microphone and Gallagher stopped moving. Within seconds he'd found himself a half-assed hiding spot and set up shop again. Red blobs were converging on her, and the pattern suggested they'd settled into an organized sweep.

"I'm up," he said.

Carmen turned slowly, giving him full view of the room. What was noted on their plans as simply a window was, in fact, a span of stained glass. It didn't open, and even if she started smashing glass, the lead would have to be dealt with, seriously hampering her exit.

Neither of them had noted that detail during her earlier search of the room and now she was well and truly fucked.

Gallagher took one breath, and everything outside of the handheld screen and his objective fell away. Steer the green dot through the maze without making contact with the red blobs, one life left and no more quarters.

Carmen listened to Gallagher breathe while retrieving her

13

weapon from the pocket on her thigh. It was only a .22, nothing like the other agents carried, but she rarely needed a firearm. She liked her .22, was highly proficient with it thanks to range time, and now she felt a hell of a lot safer with it in her hands.

The incriminating diary was secured in her jumpsuit, in a specially made pocket that stretched from her waist to just below her shoulder blades so as not to hamper her movement. Various other pockets held essential tools of the trade. Unlike Gallagher, she traveled unencumbered by a pack.

A few more seconds ticked away and Carmen moved to a ready position at the door. Random thoughts went through her head—with the exception of the office, the doors in the house all stood open. How had they missed the stained glass? Was the interior wired for video?

Then she willfully blanked her mind. Gallagher might be an overbearing Neanderthal, but he was also a mission-planning god. No matter how desperate a situation seemed, obeying Gallagher with no hesitation and no second-guessing substantially increased a person's chances of survival.

"On my go, exit into hall left, one-point-five meters, enter door on right." A long pause. "Go."

Carmen went, moving silently in custom, soft-soled boots.

"Hold."

She was in an interior room with no other means of exit but the door she'd come in.

"On my go, exit hall right, at T go right, three meters, door on left. On the double quick."

She realized they were in a tight cat and mouse game and Gallagher was keeping her one room—or maybe even literally one step—ahead of the cats.

"Go."

She sprinted to the hallway junction, banged a right and slid into the room just as a glimpse of movement appeared at the other end. *Close.*

A window.

"Weapons?"

".22."

"Suppressed?"

"Ten seconds." She kept her voice almost nonexistent, knowing the sensitive mic of her comm would pick it up. Her hand was already on her right thigh pocket, sliding open the well-lubricated, silent zipper.

"Acknowledged."

Carmen threaded the silencer onto the end of the barrel.

"Isolated target approaching from left, ETA twenty seconds."

She tapped twice on her mic.

"Ten seconds to door."

Even suppressed, the ballistic crack wouldn't go unnoticed, but it would make it harder to pinpoint her location. The target never knew what hit him.

"Target down," she reported. "Window?"

"Negative. Guy on the ground. *Shit.*"

That wasn't what a girl wanted Gallagher whispering in her earpiece. "Since we were never here, telling the Feds about the diary won't do shit. At least get me to a place I can toss it to you. Get it out of here."

"I'm getting *you* out, so just don't lose it."

"Not to get pushy, but that shot had to have attracted some attention. I need to move."

"I think things are about to get worse. It looks like the staff is evacuating through the kitchen and the goons seem to be retreating."

She felt a brief, stupid moment of relief before the bigger picture developed in her mind. "Are they going to smoke me out?"

"Smoke we can deal with. A big boom we can't."

"You think they'll blow this place? You're talking millions and—"

"Think how much he stands to lose. Not just financial, but political ruin."

"How long until they've cleared the building?"

"Not long enough. And you having free run of the house does no good if they're outside waiting. I'm monitoring on the move now, circling."

"There's a pool," she said.

"No diving board, so I'm not chancing it being deep enough for that kind of jump."

She could hear the whisper of his breath grow slightly more ragged. Considering his physical conditioning, he must have been seriously hauling ass through the woods.

"The garage," he shouted, and she winced as it echoed around her eardrum.

"We don't know what's in there, since we didn't search it yet. And with the freakin' computers in high-end cars nowadays, I'm shit out of luck hotwiring unless he's got a classic stowed in there."

"The floor plan shows six doors—three in the front and three in the back so they can drive in, then drive out. Two sets are significantly smaller than the third."

"Snowmobiles."

"If I throw up a distraction, you can punch out of there and

16

you'll be hard as hell to hit."

"One, I've got to get the door open and two, most of the snow's gone. There's none around the house."

"It'll be sketchy on the garage floor, but as soon as you're free of the cement it'll fly. Just like the grass drags."

What the hell was he talking about? "Grass drags?"

"They're almost clear of the house. Get to the garage and let me know when you're there."

It took her almost a full minute because the house was big and she thought it wise to be cautious since he couldn't monitor his screen and run through the woods at the same time. He talked to her the entire time.

"The good news—I think they're going to smoke you out rather than blow you up," he said. "Bad news—they've set up a pretty tight perimeter and I'm on the outside of it. You can't start a two-stroke on the QT, so no fucking around. You fire it, then go like hell. Straight shot thirty yards across the grass, clear trail into the woods.

"Sixty yards in, then a sharp right turn. You blow that, you're fucked. Another twenty-five yards, the trail dips into a gully. Leave it running. I dropped my pack there, so grab it, then sit way back on the seat. I'll be coming hard, and then you stick yourself to me like we're one person. And listen up, because this is important."

As if thirty wide-open yards and becoming one with a tree weren't? "I'm listening."

"When you come out the door, I'll be to your right. Once you clear the door I won't be able to shoot across you, so you need to lean down over the gas tank—make yourself a smaller target—and keep your head lowered to the right because I'll be covering that side."

17

"Wrap my body around the gas tank they're shooting at. Got it. Which side is the throttle on?"

"Jesus, Carmen, it's a snowmobile."

"Yeah, we rode those a lot in southern Texas."

"*Fuck.*" Again with the sweet nothings. "It's on the right. Listen, can you ride a motorcycle?"

"Yes."

"Instead of turning the grip, there's a thumb lever, and no shifting—the higher you rev it, the faster it goes. Other than that, close enough."

Carmen cautiously entered the garage and found it empty but for a truck and four snowmobiles. "I'm here. Four machines, all facing the right direction. Keys in them."

"Good. Saves time yanking the ignition. Describe the floor."

"Cement, but there's a rubber track under the machines that extends to the doors."

"You won't spin the track trying to take off. Tell me about the machines closest to the doors."

One was a bad-ass looking sport model, the other a comfortable two-seater. Since she wasn't embarking on a Sunday drive, Carmen wasn't surprised when he passed on the touring model.

"How, exactly," she asked, "am I supposed to get through a closed door?"

Chapter Two

From his treetop vantage point, Gallagher swept his binoculars across the property. Now that the perimeter was established and they were confident the intruder couldn't escape, they had slowed things down. The men were waiting, calming themselves and coming up with a plan.

Gallagher just had to come up with a better plan faster and he and Carmen would win.

The garage door was a problem. As he took a few precious minutes to recover from reconning her escape route and his position at warp speed, he came up with options and discarded them just as quickly.

"There's a helmet in here," she said. "Can the machine just punch through the door?"

"Negative. You screw up your skis and you're either stranded in the open or in a tree."

"I could hit the button, then fire the machine. House this nice, the door runners will be smooth and quiet."

"Two guys with direct view of both doors."

"Shoot them first."

Nice that she had that much faith in his aim. "Is the garage heated?"

"Yes. Feels like the same temp as the house."

"Thank God for spoiled rich people. The sled'll fire right up."

"I'm sitting on it now, looking it over, getting a feel for it."

Gallagher wiped the sweat from his forehead and took a few deep breaths. This wasn't the worst situation he'd ever been in, but was possibly the first time he hadn't been prepared for the possibility of this kind of screw-up. A sneak and peak. Nobody but a skeleton household crew.

What the hell had gone wrong?

Having familiarized himself with the surrounding community before the job, he knew enough time had passed so he'd hear sirens if they'd called the cops. The fact they hadn't meant they were going to handle Carmen themselves.

Gallagher knew one thing for damn sure—if they got Carmen he was going to shoot as many of the motherfuckers as he had bullets for before they got him, too.

"I'm ready when you are," Carmen said.

He took a deep breath. The men were starting to get antsy—they'd go on the offensive soon. But, god-*damn*-it, he wished there were some other way to do this. Some way that kept Carmen out of the line of fire.

But he hadn't packed for this kind of cluster fuck and now she'd be out in the open on a machine she maybe couldn't handle.

"Walk through it for me, babe."

"Hit the button, run to the machine, turn the key, stay low, head to the right, punch it and go. Thirty yards to the tree line, sixty yards to the corner, twenty-five yards to the rendezvous."

"That's my girl."

"And don't call me babe."

"If it doesn't fire the first time, you go back inside and hide yourself."

"Affirmative."

"When you're ready, give me a countdown to go on the button, then haul ass, babe."

"Three...two...one..."

Deep breath.

"Go."

The snowmobile fired, roaring to life in a cloud of oily smoke and Carmen launched, barely clearing the door crawling its way upward.

The chill seared her skin and made her eyes tear up, but she'd seen the break in the trees and kept the nose pointed in that direction.

She heard the gunfire—Gallagher's shots louder in her earpiece—heard some *thwaps* against the machine. Doing damn near a hundred already, she didn't dare to flinch.

A bullet would either knock her off the sled or it wouldn't.

She made the tree line. Panicked at the trees making blurry boundaries down both sides. The snow was icier in the shade— the machine went squirrelly on her.

Carmen eased off the throttle, let the snowmobile right itself.

The corner came up fast. She took her thumb off the throttle, but it wasn't enough. Grabbed the brakes and it locked up, sliding into the corner.

She swore and released the brakes, hit the throttle again, letting the weight carry it through.

Then she punched it again, screaming through a gap in the trees not much wider than the machine.

Finally the trail dropped into a low spot and she stopped. Blinking away the tears her eyes summoned to protect them from the wind, she left the machine running and climbed off. Her legs were a little rubbery, but she found Gallagher's pack and slipped her arms through the straps. Then she went back to the machine, pushing herself back on the seat as far as she could.

With the engine at idle and the wind no longer rushing past, she could hear Gallagher's ragged breath in her earpiece. He was running fast.

"I'm here," she said, just so he knew he was running toward something.

Barely thirty seconds later she caught movement in the trees and reached for her gun.

It was Gallagher, his face nearly as red with exertion as the side of his lightweight coat was with blood. He'd been hit.

"You're wounded," she said as he slid onto the seat in front of her. "Place my hand so I'm not squeezing it."

As she shoved forward so her body was plastered against his, he took her arms and wrapped them low on his abdomen, below the wound.

Then the machine roared and they were flying down the trail. Carmen forced herself to become boneless against his back, offering no resistance as he leaned in the corners.

His body was hot and every time she inhaled her senses were overwhelmed by the scent of sweat and fresh blood.

"Shit!"

Carmen jerked her head up and dared a look over his shoulder.

A pond. Not a very big one, but there was no trail around it. They had to go over it.

Too bad it wasn't frozen anymore.

"Don't panic, babe!" he shouted into her earpiece, and then he pegged the throttle. "Like glue now, and *don't lean!*"

What the hell did it matter if she leaned since they were about to crash and—assuming they didn't die on impact— drown, but she kept her arms low on his waist and did the boneless leech thing again.

She felt the jolt of the machine hitting the water, but the dumb son of a bitch driving never let off the throttle.

"Come on, baby, skim," he said, but she realized he was talking to the snowmobile and closed her eyes.

She didn't need to see anything. Frigid water rushing into her lungs would be warning enough he'd failed.

Incredibly, she felt the skis jolt and Gallagher let off the throttle, but she never got wet. He just kept going down the trail.

A few minutes later, when they came out into a back street in town, Gallagher didn't slow down. The picks on the snowmobile's track bit into the asphalt, but he navigated to the airport, across the field and straight to the helicopter.

"Let's blow this joint," he said, and she pulled her earpiece. She didn't need him in stereo.

He was a little slow getting off the machine, and she felt a jolt of anxiety. "Can you fly?"

"It's just a flesh wound. You can slap a bandage on it once we're up."

"Let's go, then, before they catch up."

"You got it, babe."

"Don't call me babe."

When Alex Rossi stepped out of the house, he found his wife still trying to master the art of climbing into their new hammock without spinning out and landing on her face.

Grace hit the ground with a thump—again—but he didn't laugh this time. He didn't even crack a smile.

She noticed immediately. "Is it Danny?"

Their son was doing Disney with her parents. Alex shook his head. "Charlotte just called. Gallagher and Carmen...the chopper went down in the White Mountains."

"Oh shit." She pushed herself to her feet and started across the yard to him. "Do we know anything?"

"Just that it crashed."

"We'll take the Hummer. The gear bags are packed in the hall closet, but double-check for the sat phone and radios. Cell phone coverage up there sucks. Grab the cold-weather bags out of the basement—they're blue. I'll change and meet you out front in five."

Alex shoved his hands through his hair. "You don't have to go, Grace. You don't do this stuff anymore."

"It stopped being a Devlin Group mission when they went down. Now your best friend *and* my best friend are out there, hopefully still alive and waiting for us to come and get them."

God, he hoped they were alive. "Then you're down to four minutes, sweetheart. Move your ass."

It was pitch black, and Gallagher couldn't tell if it was the lack of a moon or the blood in his eyes.

It was quiet—too damn quiet—and he wondered if he'd gone deaf, too. Did he have a concussion? Hell, was he dead?

The crash. They'd gone down. A loud *popping* sound. Smoke. Then everything totally went to shit. The helicopter out of control. Carmen trying to signal a Mayday and getting nobody. Scrambling to get her comm link to Charlotte back up.

Fighting for control of the bird. Managing to achieve autorotation so they didn't drop like a rock. Adjusting the collective pitch. Telling Carmen... *Shit.* He hadn't meant to tell her that.

He'd thought, for a second, he'd put her down in one piece, but the tail rotor caught on...something. A tree? They'd spun and then it all went black.

"Carmen?" he whispered, and though it came out little more than a croak, Gallagher was relieved he could hear it.

He tried to work some moisture into his mouth and licked his lips, only to taste blood there, as well. And a fresh cut that hurt like hell. He wasn't dead. *Shit.*

And Carmen hadn't answered him. Time to get his ass in gear. His arms and legs seemed to work, and if he squinted he could make out a sliver of light to his left. So he wasn't blind, nor had he been unconscious into nightfall. Just buried in the rubble.

It seemed to take forever for him to unearth himself from the wreckage, his body moving like a ninety-year-old arthritic woman's, but he kept at it. Carmen could be bleeding out while he was maneuvering through jagged metal and smashed seats. He didn't allow himself to consider she might already be dead.

Gallagher blinked when the full afternoon sun pierced his throbbing head, and it was a few seconds before he saw anything but dancing spots.

They'd crashed in the White Mountains of New Hampshire, a mountain range known for claiming and concealing its victims like some kind of sub-zero Bermuda freakin' Triangle.

Well...*shit.*

The forest was still silent and, though Gallagher strained to listen, he couldn't hear anybody moving around. Finally he heard a vicious blue streak of Spanish and damn near laughed out loud.

Until he saw her. Then he made his aching body run.

Carmen Olivera had never been so cold. Even during that February job in Moscow, she hadn't lost gross motor control like this. She thought she was moving her feet the correct way, but she kept falling down. If she ever figured out what she was doing wrong, the guy who'd screwed with their helicopter was going to be one sorry bastard.

Speaking of sorry bastards, why the hell was Gallagher running and yelling at her? Maybe she should duck.

Instead, she fell. Again. Then he started dragging her, and Carmen wanted to protest, but even her mouth was starting to act up on her now.

He dumped her on the ground next to a flickering-out engine fire and she blinked slowly. When he started ripping up seats like a madman, she got concerned. Maybe he'd hit his head.

Ooh, he was making a fire. That was nice. Maybe they could roast marshmallows later and sing "Kumbaya". If she could remember the words.

What a lot of trees there were. She should be able to find a nice marshmallow stick. When she woke up from her nap, maybe. Since her arms and legs didn't work so well anymore, she closed her eyes.

But Gallagher was yelling at her again. He really was a pain in the ass sometimes.

Such a fine-looking pain in the ass, though. All tall and muscled. Shaggy gold hair she always wanted to run her fingers through. But she didn't because...why didn't she?

And those blue eyes and that naughty grin. They always made her want to take her clothes off, so she tried not to look at him.

When he started tearing her shirt off her body, Carmen thought about protesting again. So very caveman of him. But her head lolled back and she was looking at the trees again.

The fire was really big now, and Gallagher's hands were warm.

Oooh, she was naked.

Had his grin finally made her clothes fall off? No. He had on his big, bad warrior look.

There was blood on his face.

Where were the marshmallows?

Operation Getting Carmen Naked had been in the planning stages for a long time, but the original mission parameters had called for her being a lot more awake and a little less frigid.

After Hell Week, SEAL service and eleven years with the Devlin Group, Gallagher would never have imagined the hardest thing he'd ever do was get a wet sports bra over the head of an uncooperative woman while trying not to look at her breasts.

Not that he didn't want to see them, but ogling a half-frozen, unconscious woman would make him a sick bastard. Plus she kept muttering something about finding a sharp stick, and he wanted no part of that.

Once he was done doing battle with the spandex or whatever from hell, he laid her down on the emergency blanket from his pack he'd spread in a snow-free spot. Then he wiped the sweat from his forehead with the sleeve of his coat.

Bottom half next.

Jesus.

Two minutes with his eyes closed, then he was able to cover her with a second emergency blanket scavenged from the on-board first aid kit.

"S'mores?"

At least, that's what he *thought* she'd said. "No s'mores, babe."

No food of any kind, unless somebody had snacks stowed away on the helo somewhere. Never again would he pack light. *Simple sneak and peek, my ass.*

He pulled off his coat and folded it up to put under her head, trying to figure out what to do with her hair. She wore it in a tight, thick braid when she worked, and it was up away from her face and neck. But it would probably take a lot longer to dry that way and a damp scalp wasn't going to help her any.

As gently as he could, Gallagher pulled the elastic from her hair and started separating the strands. He loved her hair. It was dark and long and straight, like the liquid chocolate he'd seen pouring over some fancy fountain thing once.

Once he got the three strands separated, he used his fingertips to spread her hair up over his coat, away from her skin. She made a low, sexy as hell *mmmmm* sound deep in her throat, and he forced his body not to get too excited.

He tried, anyway.

She was starting to shiver, though, so he quit playing with her hair and quickly checked her for other injuries. By strategically shifting the blanket around, he gave her a semblance of privacy, and he was relieved to find she was in roughly the same shape he was, minus the gunshot wound.

Bruised all to hell, with numerous and abrasions and minor lacerations, but nothing life threatening. No broken bones. No evidence of a head injury.

It was nothing short of a miracle, he thought as he tossed some more scavenged fuel onto the fire. Then he arranged some scrap metal from the helicopter around her to reflect the fire before covering the half-ass shelter with evergreen branches to hold the heat down.

As he slid between the two blankets and pulled Carmen into his embrace—just for body heat, of course—he considered their next move.

He'd been flying helicopters a long damn time, and he knew sabotage when he saw it. A fucking EMP, no less, because every electronic device they had was totally dead. Since they weren't emitting a signal, it might be a very long time before anybody found them.

They might not have a very long time in these conditions. Spring came late to the mountains, and they weren't prepared for an extended cold-weather camping trip.

When Carmen sighed and relaxed against his body, he tightened his arms around her. There was no way in hell he was going to let her be a statistic, no matter what the odds stacked against him.

The Devlin Group had never lost an agent on Gallagher's watch, and the first for damn sure wouldn't be Carmen.

Chapter Three

In the time it took them to tear up the highway to the Notch, Alex and Grace kept the phone lines humming.

Danny wasn't due back for three days, but Alex listened to her fill her mother in on the situation. Then she called Charlotte again.

Charlotte Rhames was executive administrative assistant to Alex in title, but in reality she was the grease that made the Group's wheels turn. She was a dynamo, brilliant, and had the remarkable ability to run herd on high-strung contract agents spread out all over the planet. She also paid more in taxes than the president each year and was worth every single penny Alex paid her.

She was in the process of relocating from NYC to Texas, where she was currently in Bridezilla mode for her upcoming marriage to Tony Casavetti. But there was no mention of gowns or flowers as her voice blasted through the Hummer's speakers.

"I've sent the location of the Search and Rescue staging area to your GPS. Scott Denton is in charge and on site. No signal from the helicopter—it was either deactivated or destroyed. A Fish & Game officer heard the explosion so, while they can't pinpoint, there's a very vague general direction.

"I provided a Canadian contact with rushed press creds and she said a man with a bloody shirt and a woman came out of the woods on a snowmobile and were speeding down the streets. With multiple witnesses pieced together, it sounds like they were headed for the airport."

"Something went wrong at Arceneau's." Rossi pounded the steering wheel. "Dammit, why didn't we have audio on them?"

"It was a basic sneak and peek, Alex. A waste of tech man-hours is what we decided."

He'd decided it, actually, but she was being nice to him. "We're going to touch base with S&R and if nothing's moving, I'm going to go have a look-see across the border. Find the closest airport to the staging area and have a helicopter on stand-by."

"Will do."

"And I don't care what you have to monitor or how you do it, but that bastard Arceneau doesn't leave the country."

Carmen couldn't believe she'd been stupid enough to fall asleep in a sauna. And judging by the lingering grogginess and her languid muscles, she'd been out for a while—long enough to start dehydrating.

The awareness came slowly that not only was she naked, but a body was spooned around hers. A very hard, male body.

At least he wasn't naked, too.

"Carm?" the hard, male body said in Gallagher's voice and memories of the day slammed into her—right up to the point she'd told herself to get up out of the water and move or she'd die.

"This is interesting," she said softly.

"You must have landed in a brook or something, because you were soaked to the skin and hypothermia was setting in."

She looked around at the shelter he'd thrown together from helicopter pieces and fallen trees, then at the very healthy fire heating the space. "Well, you fixed the hell out of that, didn't you?"

"I might have overdone it a bit," he admitted. "I thought you were going to die on me."

And just like that the memory of their last seconds before impact popped into her brain.

"This isn't how I wanted to die."

"Since it doesn't look good, I may as well tell you—I've wanted to make love to you since the first time I saw you."

Then their world had exploded.

She shivered now, remembering the low, intense timbre of his voice, so different from his usual surfer-boy ease. He must have thought her still cold because he pulled her even tighter against his body.

"I'm guessing my clothes didn't fall off in the crash."

"They should be dry by now. I'll get them in a minute."

She tried to inch away. "You could have left my underwear."

"You were soaked through. I didn't get off on it, if that's what you're worried about. I thought you were dying."

"I'm not, so do me a favor and toss me my clothes."

She almost regretted the demand when he got up and the chill set in. Even when he wasn't overheated from exertion, his body was like a hot water bottle.

After pulling on her clothes, she sat cross-legged on one of the two torn, slightly singed cushions he hadn't fed to the fire while Gallagher turned his attention to one of the helicopter's metal storage boxes. It must have broken loose, and it was so dented he was struggling to open it.

"How long until S&R comes, do you think?" she asked.

"You'd be surprised how hard it is to find a downed aircraft in these mountains." The storage box finally gave and a cache of granola bars spilled out. "Could be five hours or five years."

Carmen grabbed a bar and peeled back the wrapper while Gallagher put half of the bars into his pack. "Have a plan yet?"

"I'm going to see if I can find a trail—cross country skiing or snowmobile—or maybe a hunting cabin. Just keep the fire going the way it is and stay close to it. You'll be fine until I get back."

It took a few seconds for his words to register. And to realize he intended to leave her behind. "You're not going without me."

Gallagher zipped the bag—now she knew why he'd only packed half the bars—then grabbed a cushion and parked himself next to her. "I can move faster without you, babe."

"I can keep up with you in my sleep, so don't give me that bullshit. And what if you don't come back?"

He looked at her as though she'd just sprouted a second head. "Of course I'll come back. Why the hell wouldn't I?"

Because the only thing worse than being stranded in the cold mountains was being stranded alone, and with the way her luck was running, she didn't want to take the chance.

"What if you get lost?" she asked, and he snorted. "What if you get hurt and freeze to death in a snowbank? What if you cross a really pissed-off bear?"

"Then you keep the fire going, boil water, ration your food and wait for S&R."

If he were a physically weaker man, she'd strangle him where he sat. "You're the one who said it could be five hours to five years before they find the chopper."

Gallagher growled and scrubbed his hands over his face. "You're a pain in the ass, woman."

"If you don't come back I'm screwed anyway, so I may as well go with you."

Judging by his expression, he'd rather shoot himself in the foot, but Carmen didn't care. There was no way in hell she was spending the night alone in the woods with God only knew what rabid and ravenous wildlife. She'd be in full nervous breakdown mode within an hour.

"Afraid of the dark, babe?" he teased, but she was on to his game. He thought he could shame her into staying alone.

Well, that wasn't happening. She'd cry and wring her hands like a helpless little girl if she had to, but she wasn't playing Goldilocks to any freakin' bears.

Alex Rossi had only known Scott Denton ten minutes and he already wanted to strangle him. Not enough to kill him. Just enough to get his attention.

"Look, Mr. and Mrs. Rossi, what you need to do is find yourself a local motel room—that woman with the clipboard over there can give you directions—have a meal and wait for news. There's nothing you can do here."

"There sure as hell is. You've got a blank check for this op, Denton, and I can get you anything you need. You don't have enough choppers? I can get you Marine One."

Denton didn't look impressed. "This isn't a problem you can throw money at, bud. This is about experienced search and rescue personnel combing those mountains by air and on foot in the cold and the dark and the snow or rain and whatever it takes to find that helicopter."

Grace stepped up, silencing her husband with a hand on his arm. "We just want you to know if there's anything at all we can provide to support your search, please let us know."

Denton pulled off his knit cap and scrubbed his hand through his hair. "Coffee and sandwiches."

"Coffee?" Rossi could practically feel the man's pulse stuttering under his squeezing fingers. With the full resources of the Devlin Group at hand, he expected them to serve coffee?

Grace dialed her phone. "Charlotte, I need a full service coffee and deli tent at the staging area, no onsite power, staff of...three, within the hour. Thank you."

"Done," Rossi said.

Denton shook his head. "I've got to get back to work."

Less than five minutes passed before the woman with the clipboard hailed him. "Hey, Scott? I've got a twenty-by-twenty catering tent with a big-ass generator coming in twenty minutes. Where do you want it?"

He pointed, then walked back to Rossi. "I get your point. If there's something I can't get my hands on I think will help, I'll let you know."

"That's all I'm asking."

"But to be honest, I don't care if you've got the President of the United States on speed dial." As if he'd store classified numbers on a cell phone. "The only folks who can find your friends are God and my people, so stay out of our way."

Gallagher used his knife to carve an arrow into a tree. Chances were S&R would find the wreckage first and he wanted them to know where the souls on board had wandered off to.

"Tell me again why we can't stay here with the fire and the

cushions?"

He'd sell his soul for a half-foot of duct tape. Gagging her wouldn't interfere with her ability to walk. "Early spring conditions. We're comfortable now, but if we get rain during the day and then frost at night, you and I are facing hypothermia. We need dry shelter."

He adjusted his pack on his shoulders and watched her try to settle the makeshift sling pack over hers. He'd managed to salvage some first aid items, a flashlight, the emergency blankets and a screwdriver. It wasn't much, but he didn't want to leave anything behind.

"Maybe we could use the emergency blankets to make a tent."

"Not big enough." He was starting to think a certain Devlin Group agent was afraid of furry woodland creatures. "Look, babe, how many times have you trusted me with your life? How many times has my judgment meant life or death to you?"

She stared at him, her big brown eyes seeming to look for something in his face. Then she took a deep breath, nodded and settled the pack on her hip. "I'm ready."

They walked for almost five hours, stopping only to mark a tree and eat a little snow now and then. She kept up a steady pace behind him for the first two hours, but he slowed purposely after that, hoping to keep the sweat to a minimum. But as twilight fell over the woods, he noticed her starting to limp and halted.

"Let me see that pack," he said.

She handed it over without argument and sat on a fallen tree.

"Have a little more snow," he told her as he dumped the contents of the makeshift sack onto the ground. "Now that it's getting dark, you won't be able to have more. It drops your core temp."

He found a clean icy clump of his own to suck on while he sifted through his pack. Toward the bottom he found a clean pair of socks and set those aside. By discarding some of his nonessentials he was able to fit the items from the wreckage she'd been carrying into his pack.

"Take those boots off." He knew she was miserable when she did so without a knee-jerk reaction to his tone. "Shit. Cotton socks?"

He peeled them off and examined her feet. They seemed warm enough and she didn't have any blisters. Yet.

"I think they're just sore from the lack of support," she said as he massaged them. "The boots are made for stealth, not hiking."

"Wear these socks, instead. The wool will keep your feet warm, even if they get wet, and they have padded soles and some arch support. Even too big, they might help."

"I'm still good to go."

"I know you are, babe. But from here on out, you keep me informed of *any* changes in your physical condition."

"Aye aye, sir." She snapped him a smart salute.

He laughed and helped her slip her boots back on before reshouldering the pack. The extra items didn't add a lot of weight, but it didn't take much to throw someone as small as Carmen even a little off balance. The effects added up with the miles.

"You can't carry everything, Gallagher. It wasn't my back bothering me."

"I know, but this is better. I'd like to go another two hours or to some kind of shelter—whichever comes first."

"Or the batteries run out in the flashlight."

"True. As soon as we find a good place I'll get a fire started."

Not ten minutes later, Gallagher found what looked to be a deliberately cut trail through the woods. It hadn't been traveled recently, but it was there for a reason.

Since the horizon was cloaked in darkness, he scouted around for a place to camp. The stars were out, so rain probably wouldn't be a concern.

"I thought we were going on," Carmen said when he dropped his pack.

"I want to stay on this trail, but I need to make sure we're headed down the mountain. First light, I'll point us in the right direction."

He built them a fire and they split a granola bar. Then there was nothing to do but curl up between the silver emergency blankets. Carmen stunned him by not only accepting his arms around her, but actually snuggling against him. Not that he was complaining.

"You're like an electric blanket I don't have to plug in," she mumbled, and then her body went lax as sleep hit her hard.

As tired as he was, sleep eluded Gallagher for a long time.

Carmen walked. And walked and walked some more.

Gallagher had given her an entire granola bar, folded the blanket and then set off in what he claimed was the right direction.

They didn't expend energy on small talk. Not that they were a pair with much to talk about, but speaking would at least have broken the monotony of her own thoughts.

She wasn't afraid, per se. Working with the Devlin Group had thrown a lot of things more dangerous than being lost in the woods at her. And with Gallagher two steps in front of her and Rossi out there hunting for them, she wouldn't be lost long.

No, what scared the crap out of her was the solo time with Gallagher. She'd invested too much time in keeping her distance to start cuddling up at night with him now. If she got too comfortable, she might give in and once she did, they could never go back again. There would only be forward or apart. Apart would ruin their working relationship.

But forward would eventually lead to a dead end. She'd known Gallagher a long time and, even though he didn't give specifics, she'd figured out family was everything to him. He was the kind of guy who just naturally assumed his future would include a white picket fence, two or three kids, and a golden retriever wearing fake reindeer antlers in the annual Christmas photo.

Carmen wasn't wired for Christmas card photos and cute dogs. The realities of parenthood had sent her father screaming into the night—he'd lasted two months. Her mother died when she was ten and she'd been placed in the first of many foster homes she'd been shuffled to.

It wasn't being in the system that had turned her off having a family, though. She hadn't been abused or mistreated, or even neglected. No great trauma there.

She just didn't feel that maternal drive. Some women—like Grace—were great mothers, but Carmen didn't even have the urge to try. Even in her most introspective moments, there was no biological clock ticking in the shadows. And she'd bet the idea of a woman not wanting a family would be an alien concept to Gallagher.

She almost laughed at herself. It was a big jump from huddling together for warmth to pushing a baby carriage.

"Here," he said, jerking her out of her thoughts.

"Here what?"

He gestured up at the sky. "It's going to rain soon and, judging by the change already, it's going to be colder tonight. We need to stay as dry as possible."

As he talked he was rearranging the thick, overlapping branches of several close juniper trees, weaving them so they formed a makeshift roof. When he was done, he fed one silver blanket into one of the layers to help waterproof it and spread the other on the ground.

"How long do you think it'll rain?"

"Hopefully just a passing shower, and then we'll push on."

She hoped so. As hard as the walking was, it was still easier than being squeezed into a tight shelter with Gallagher. The wall she'd built around her attraction for him was eroding faster than she could patch it, and his body wrapped around hers was a giant, swinging wrecking ball she couldn't seem to avoid.

Chapter Four

"Looks like a hunter's cabin," Gallagher said in a low voice as they peeked through the branches. "The snow's undisturbed, so I don't think anybody's been here for a while."

Still, he signaled for her to approach cautiously, watching for any sign of movement in the shack or in what he assumed was an outhouse behind it. The door wasn't locked and it took less than a minute to clear the single room.

"Thank God for woodstoves," Carmen said, already on her knees in front of it. "I'll start small to test the flue—see if anything's nesting in it—but then watch out."

While she worked on getting them warm, Gallagher lit the kerosene lamp in the center of the small table and took stock of their situation.

No radio. No well pump, so they'd be boiling snow on the woodstove. One ancient looking twin bed and an oversized armchair that might have sat on the side of some road somewhere for quite a while before the new owner saved it. No fridge or icebox. Half a jar of instant coffee and about two dozen packages of Ramen in a variety of flavors.

"Huh." Carmen looked over his shoulder. "He could have stocked some chili or some beef stew."

"Cans freeze, they could explode. Messy and it attracts things you don't want attracted."

"At least we're all set with our daily sodium requirements."

Gallagher didn't give a damn about their salt intake. He'd gotten her out of the cold, and that was all that mattered. She was bruised, battered, and her feet probably hurt like hell, but she was alive and she was going to stay that way.

As warmth began to curl out from the woodstove, the tension Gallagher had carried through everything—getting her away from Arceneau's men, the crash, the cold woods, the forced air of unerring confidence required to lead people through hell—began to melt away and he sagged against the short counter.

They weren't out of danger, by any means. Even if he managed to snare or hunt some small game, their food supply was exhaustible, as was the cured wood. And he wasn't lying when he said it could be years before the wreckage was found. It wasn't unheard of in the White Mountains.

He didn't have to the heart to tell her yet but, since he wasn't willing to take the chance, they wouldn't be staying long.

Alex Rossi walked into the shabby office of the airport Gallagher and Carmen had departed from with his wife at his side. He was worried, tired, pissed and visibly armed.

The pencilneck running the place squealed when Rossi went around the counter, grabbed him by the throat and threw him into his chair. "Helicopter flew in today, worked fine, didn't when it left. Why?"

"I don't know what you're—"

Rossi hit him. Just a backhand, but it snapped the guy's head back and split his lip. Bob—so the tag on his shirt said—tasted blood and started to shake.

"Don't fuck with me, Bob."

"I'm not! Man, I can't...I didn't..."

He hit him again. "You did. Now tell me about it."

Grace unfolded her knife and made a show of cleaning her fingernails. Bob started making a high-pitched wheezing sound, his gaze jerking between the blade and Rossi.

"I have a list of call numbers—you know, the registration numbers on an aircraft?"

Rossi nodded. "And my helicopter's call number was on that list?"

Bob's Adam's apple had been bouncing like a sing-along dot, and now his head joined in.

"So what did you do then?"

Bob's eyes widened and the smell of his fear was as ripe as rotting garbage. He opened his mouth, then closed it again.

"Look, Bob. You're afraid whoever gave you that list *might* come and kill you if you talk to me." The nodding intensified. "But I'm already here and there's no *might* about it. I *will* kill you."

He thought he heard Grace snort, but Bob didn't seem to notice, so Rossi didn't bother glaring at her.

"I had to call a number and give the guy who answered the call number. That's it, I swear."

Rossi leaned forward, crowding him. "That's not it. What happened next?"

"Somebody drove out here and...I dunno. Double-checked the call number is what I figured."

More like planted some kind of timed explosive device. "Who gave you the list?"

"Some guy. He didn't tell me his name."

"But you know who that guy worked for, or you wouldn't have jumped when he said jump. Who?"

Bob started shaking his head, so Rossi popped him again. A little lighter this time. The poor schmuck wasn't a bad guy. He was just a chickenshit who'd let someone pull his strings.

"Where did the list come from, Bob?"

"Mr. Arceneau. Jean Arceneau." Then he burst into tears. *Shit.* Grace put her knife away.

"We're leaving now, Bob. But if my people don't come out of the woods okay, I'll be back."

They walked back to their chartered helicopter and Grace let him strap in before she laughed. "I'll be *bahk.*"

"Shut up. I didn't say it like that."

"Poor Bob's never going to watch *Terminator* again without pissing himself."

As the sun went down and the outside grew cold, Carmen decided she'd be perfectly happy never leaving the cabin again.

She was safe, warm and had a belly full of Ramen, which gave at least the illusion of being well-fed. After being shot at, nearly drowning on a snowmobile, surviving a helicopter crash and a grueling trek through the woods, what else did a girl really need?

Gallagher entered the cabin in a swirl of a light snow flurry carried on the wind. "It's getting colder."

"That's why I quit drinking anything two hours ago. I'd rather not make another trip to the outhouse."

He flashed a grin at her and she couldn't help returning it. He'd changed almost the minute they'd stepped into the cabin— morphing back into the laid-back beach bum persona they all knew and put up with.

When he threw his coat over the hook by the door and then hauled his T-shirt over his head, she stopped smiling but didn't look away. The bandage over the gunshot wound needed to be changed, and he'd manage to acquire quite the additional collection of cuts and bruises during their adventures. "Let me clean that for you. I can boil some strips of cloth for fresh bandages."

He waved away her concern. "Tomorrow, when we have decent light. For now I just want to crash."

Carmen dragged the chair cushions onto the floor, wrapped herself in a blanket that smelled like wet dog and curled up on top of them.

"You're taking the bed," Gallagher said in his brooking-no-arguments tone.

"Doesn't look that way." She opened her eyes to find him glaring down at her, arms crossed over his chest. She might have been intimidated if she wasn't too busy admiring what the position did to his biceps. "Look, you carried everything *and* broke trail through the snow. If we have to walk more, you're going to do it again. You being well-rested is more important. Life or death, even."

Sounded logical enough. Clearly he thought so, too, because after a few more seconds of staring he blew out the lamp and stretched out on the old mattress.

Then he groaned.

"Oh, and it sags like a son of a bitch in the middle."

His swearing and the squeaks and pops as he tried to get comfortable nearly drowned out her laughter.

"Rossi," he barked into the phone, picturing Charlotte rolling her eyes. She claimed he watched too much television.

"Arceneau's in custody—get this, he turned himself in—and he's demanding a sit-down with you."

"It won't help. If he's looking to sue us for the B&E, give him Grace's number. She'll talk him out of it."

Charlotte didn't laugh. "I did a preliminary with the Feds, and they want you to talk to him, too. Arceneau got mixed up in this because his daughter was kidnapped and this was the ransom."

Shit. "And the Feds want us to retrieve her."

"We get her out and he'll roll over on everybody and everything. If not, he's mum and the only evidence against him went down with the helicopter. Maybe we'll find it, maybe we won't."

"And maybe he's lying."

"He's not. There's evidence to support his claim. And once the chain is broken because he's in custody, they'll kill her."

"Don't do this to me, Charlotte." He wanted to beat his head against the nearest tree. "Things are moving here and—"

"There's a lot of pressure, Alex. This is huge and the government is ready to put their relationship with the Group on the line."

"Who has her, and where?"

"Isabelle Arceneau is being held by Le Roux himself, at his compound in Matunisia."

Holy. Shit. "We are so fucked."

"That would be an affirmative."

Carmen wasn't laughing the next morning when she woke to find herself in Gallagher's arms. Again.

At some point during the night he'd dragged the mattress down onto the floor next to her cushions and they'd met at the junction. She told herself to move—to get up and start the water boiling—but her body didn't get the memo.

She'd been fighting this thing with Gallagher for a long time. She deserved a few minutes curled against him, his chest warm against her back and his arm holding her close.

Because she wasn't in a position to overprotect him like he could her, she thought she'd done a better job of hiding her attraction than he had. But it was always there, smoldering like a burning ember she absolutely couldn't fan into a flame. If that happened, they'd both get burned.

They were probably the least compatible people on the face of the planet, and going into a relationship so obviously doomed had the potential to destroy their working relationship. Since the Group was her entire life and Gallagher was number two on the totem pole, she kept her fantasies to herself and her zipper zipped.

"You're thinking too hard," the fantasy himself mumbled into her hair. "The wheels grinding woke me up."

Now it was definitely time to get up. "I should stoke the fire."

"I'm warm enough." He nuzzled closer as if to prove his point. "Few more minutes."

"Okay, but only because we both stink and the morning breath will keep you from trying anything."

"Our stink cancels each other out."

"Behave yourself, Gallagher."

"John."

"What?"

"I'd rather you call me John. That's my name."

"John Gallagher?"

"Close enough."

He'd been just Gallagher for so long, it didn't sound right. "So you trust me enough to sleep with me, but not enough to tell me your real name?"

"Sleeping with you doesn't count when we actually sleep. And it's McLaine. John Gallagher McLaine."

She didn't want to call him John. It was too personal—a piece of himself that didn't factor into their professional relationship. Carmen the DG agent called him Gallagher. Carmen the woman currently cradled in his arms would call him John.

"I hear the grinding again," he said.

"I was thinking about how much I hate instant coffee."

"But it goes so nicely with the Ramen."

"I've still got half a granola bar and I'm not sharing." It was time to put some distance between them, so Carmen rolled off the cushions and pushed herself to her feet.

They managed to blow off an hour with busy work—quick treks to the outhouse, bringing in wood, boiling water. After forcing down some breakfast, they cleaned themselves up as much as they could. Then they sat.

"What's the plan?" Carmen asked when the boredom set in after five minutes.

"We're going to keep that stovepipe puffing smoke and give Rossi forty-eight hours to find us."

"Forty-eight hours? Why not head out now? No matter how remote, there has to be some access to this cabin. We follow it out."

"Didn't your mother ever take you to the mall?"

No. Even when she'd had a mother, there was no money. "What does shopping have to do with anything?"

"First rule of the mall—if you get lost, you stay put and let Mom find you. You go roaming around, you get more lost. So we wait, just you and me, babe."

"Then why leave at all?"

"I don't suppose *because I said so* is what you want to hear?"

She laughed. "Not unless you want to choke on your own balls."

"Probably better than choking on some *other* guy's balls."

"You didn't answer my question. Why leave at all?"

"If they don't find us in forty-eight hours, they never had a clue where we were and we'll take our chances hiking out. While I could hunt, I really don't want to stay here playing house until spring."

Playing house with John Gallagher McLaine?

Not in this lifetime.

"Mr. Rossi, we've located the wreckage."

He might have stopped breathing if not for the focus-sharpening pain of Grace's fingernails digging into his palm. *Wreckage.*

Somehow a part of him had believed Gallagher found a way to bring it down intact. That he'd be found sitting next to the helicopter, hungry and cranky and looking at his watch.

"No bodies."

The world tilted and it wasn't until Grace stepped slightly

behind him, bracing him with her body, that he realized he'd almost gone down like some kind of drama queen.

"There's evidence of a campfire," Denton continued. "At some point they abandoned the crash site. My men followed their trail and have found two marked trees so far. If your people use their heads, there's a chance we'll catch up soon and bring them home."

Rossi had to clear his throat hard before he could speak. "Thank you."

"We'll be analyzing their movements—try to get the choppers up there in a more focused location—and speed up the process. Now, that's good news, but until we find them, understand they're not out of the woods, literally or figuratively. Once somebody's out there on foot, a lot of things can happen."

"I understand." They shook hands and Denton started to walk off, but Rossi called him back. "If your guys think they're getting close, make sure they call out identification. You don't want to surprise my people."

Denton chuckled. "I made a few phone calls to see who was throwing his weight into my S&R. My crews already got that warning."

Chapter Five

Gallagher was going mad. Stark raving, foaming at the mouth, speaking in tongues mad.

His body was in a constant, uncomfortable state of arousal, and there wasn't a damn thing he could do about it. He couldn't go a bout with the speed bag or even do a few punishing lengths of the pool to burn off the jittery energy.

To make matters worse, Carmen was getting antsy, too, and while he'd like to believe she was also being fried by an overload of sexual energy, he suspected she was really working herself up to saying something awkward. She kept drawing in a short breath as though she was going to speak, then changing her mind.

He was pretty sure he knew what it was and he didn't want to talk about it. Ever.

"What you said right before we crashed—" *I've wanted to make love to you since the first time I saw you.* "—did you mean that?"

Shit, he'd been right. There should be some kind of law written—anything you said while facing certain death could not be used against you if by some crazy stroke of luck you accidentally lived.

"I don't say things I don't mean, even when I'm about to kiss a rock face."

"How come you never did...I don't know...normal-type stuff guys do. Offer to buy me a drink, invite me to a movie. Ask me what a nice girl like me's doing with a crazy group like yours."

"You've never been my biggest fan."

"I bet you were clueless in the sixth grade."

It took him a second to figure that out. "Oh, the old *I'll fuck with you so you won't know I like you* trick? So you *do* like me."

"Don't get carried away."

"But do you like me like me? You know...like that?" He grinned and nudged her.

Carmen laughed and whacked him with the pillow. "My mistake. You're still *in* the sixth grade."

"Just trying to figure out where I stand." A little pink glowed on her cheekbones, intriguing him. He didn't think he'd ever seen her blush.

"Let's just say if I could take a shower right now, you'd be a very happy man."

Instead of the most insanely frustrated man on the planet. "How 'bout a rain check?"

"I'm not a pair of out-of-stock, discounted shoes."

"Hold that thought. No, hold the thought before that one." He rummaged in one of the pockets of his cargo pants and withdrew a battered pack of gum.

"You bastard! You've been withholding minty fresh breath from me this whole time?"

"Forgot about it until now." He unwrapped a piece and handed half to her. The other half he popped in his mouth. "We'll chew for one minute, then I'm going to kiss you until you can't breathe."

She stopped in mid-chew. "Are you serious?"

He set the timer on his watch. "Chew babe. Fifty-six...fifty-five..."

They both chewed.

"How much longer?" she asked with twenty-six seconds left.

"It'll beep."

It was the longest minute of his life to date. Finally the watch beeped, gum flew and Carmen met him halfway.

Her mouth was soft and burned with peppermint, and he couldn't get enough. His tongue danced over hers and he groaned when she nipped at his bottom lip.

He fell back on the bed and she went down with him, her knee nestled between his and her body stretched out on top of him.

Carmen's kisses short-circuited his brain to the point it was him who almost forgot to breathe, and he ran his hands down her back to cup her ass. She moaned into his mouth and buried her fingers in his hair. He was about to go for it, hygiene be damned, when she stopped kissing him and laid her head on his shoulder, tracing circles on his chest with her fingertips.

"Consider yourself issued a rain check," she said in a husky voice.

He wrapped his arms around her, a little surprised she seemed content to let him hold her. Somehow, he suspected Carmen was more comfortable with hot, sweaty sex than with the intimacy of cuddling, so he was going to enjoy it as long as she'd let him.

"I was so damn scared for you, babe," he said, embarrassed when his voice cracked slightly.

"I knew you'd get me out." The certainty in her voice shook him. "Although I was a little concerned when you went all

Titanic with the snowmobile."

"We didn't sink. And it's not the first time I've gone skimming." He paused for effect. "I wasn't sure it would work with two people, though."

"Smartass." She tweaked his nipple and he yelped.

"That's not part of your usual repertoire, is it?"

"I never spill sexual secrets on the first date. Or at least before getting all lathered up in a hot, steamy shower."

He closed his eyes to savor that image. "I hope they find us soon."

"Afraid we'll run out of gum?"

"No, it's too freakin' cold to keep jerking off in the outhouse."

After polishing off the last of her soup, Carmen settled in to watch Gallagher's preparations for heading out in the morning. This was their last night in the cabin, a fact she had some serious mixed feelings about.

On one hand, she was safe in the cabin. She had shelter from the cold and any bears she might piss off by accidentally waking them from their long winter naps. On the other, they couldn't stay there forever. She wanted a salad, a thick grilled pork chop and a shower. Not necessarily in that order.

Gallagher was rearranging their socks, which they'd boiled clean, on the makeshift line they'd hung in front of the stove, and she tried not to stare at his khaki-clad ass as he bent over. The pack of gum was gone, along with the minty fresh kisses.

When he was done, he settled on the cushions next to her. "They're not quite dry yet. If you don't mind shoving your feet bare into your boots to hit the outhouse, it'd be best not to put them on until we're ready to leave."

She didn't bother trying to talk him into staying longer. After several failed attempts, she'd accepted his mind was made up. "So what are we going to talk about now? We've already burned through food, movies, television and books."

He was quiet for a few moments, which made her a little nervous. Of the two, he was the talker. "Where do you see yourself in five years, Carm?"

It wasn't idle small talk. There was a deeper, underlying question in his eyes that made her look away. "You know the job. I can't even see myself in next week, never mind five years."

Since her plans for the next half-decade shouldn't factor into the redeeming of a sexual rain check, she hoped it was one of those Small Talk 101 questions he asked everybody. Getting into a heavy relationship talk while she was weakened by hormone and sodium overloads wasn't fair.

"So tell me why you left the navy," she said in a less than subtle change of subject. "You were a SEAL and you mentioned once your dad was a career sailor. Why'd you quit?"

"Boring story, but I'll tell it anyway so *you* don't have to share anything personal." He grinned to take the sting out of getting caught. "I was getting a little tired of the red tape and politics. Tripped over Rossi when he was just getting started. We were in a Middle Eastern country we weren't supposed to be in and I had to sit on him for a couple hours. Got to talking and I made the jump."

"That's it?"

"What were you expecting?"

"Knowing you, I always assumed you instigated a mutiny or beat the shit out of your commanding officer or something. Maybe did the admiral's daughter."

"The admiral's son wasn't my type. And are you implying I have a problem with authority? I've never taken a swing at

55

Rossi."

"That's different. His only rule is don't fuck things up."

"Since that's my Golden Rule, we work well together. Plus, he pays better than Uncle Sam."

"Do you ever regret it? Leaving the navy, I mean?"

"Nope. How 'bout you? You ever regret joining the Group?"

She laughed. "I wasn't exactly on the same career path as you. You were earning stripes, I was being fitted for them."

"But your jobs were probably a little less...strenuous."

"I can hold my head up now, though. Not only do I get to use my talents, but I get to challenge myself. And, as you said, the money's damn good." A cracking sound in the woods caught her attention. "Did you hear that?"

"Might be one of those furry woodland creatures you're so afraid of." She gave him a dark look and he laughed. "I'll take a peek."

"Hail the cabin!" they heard before Gallagher got to the door. "This is Roger Bright, with Search and Rescue!"

Carmen would have bet money the last thing she'd feel in this situation would be disappointment, but it was crushing, nonetheless. She looked at Gallagher and saw the same thing in his eyes.

Their vacation from reality was over, and it was time to go home.

Jack Donovan swirled the dark amber in the bottom of his mug, then forced himself to down another swallow.

The shudder made his shoulders twitch and, since it wasn't the first time, it caught the bartender's eye. "Hey, pal, you want something else? Mixed drink? Soda or something?"

No, it had to be a beer. "I'm good, thanks."

The bartender gave him a skeptical stare, then shrugged and moved on down the bar.

Donovan resumed his swirling. The stuff tasted like piss to start with, and the slow warm to room temp wasn't helping.

But he swilled it for Chris. His climbing partner since their teens, Chris Walker had—once they were of age—always toasted a good climb with a foaming mug of whatever the local bar had on tap.

Donovan continued the tradition in honor of his friend— one beer on every anniversary of the climb that ended with Chris in a body bag. The day the gear had failed and Jack hadn't been able to hold him.

This was his third beer and he could still see that instant of awareness in Chris's eyes—the split second he realized his hand had wrenched free from Jack's and his life was over.

Another swallow of beer. Another shudder.

He didn't celebrate his own climbs anymore. There weren't any to celebrate. He hadn't managed an ascent since the day he'd dropped Chris, and at some point he'd quit trying. The fear was too much to overcome—the sweat, the tremors and the god-awful flashbacks. Giving up was easier.

His cell buzzed and he swore when he saw Rossi's name on the caller ID screen. What good was putting in for a goddamn personal day if the boss called?

He set the phone next to his beer. Pretty fucking sad when a guy couldn't be left alone to drown his sorrows in piss-poor brewski.

God, he was tired. He scrubbed his face with his palms and tried not to catch his reflection in the bar mirror.

Ghosts sucked and Chris's never came alone. No, he had to dredge up the memory of every person Donovan had let down and drag them along, too. Not everything the Devlin Group did was heavy shit. There were always secrets to learn and stolen items to recover and bodies to guard, but lives were at stake often enough to lose some.

Those losses chipped away at a man's soul. Donovan didn't have much left.

Lately, those he'd saved weren't enough to drive back the ghosts anymore. After nine years with the Group and years of undercover Vice before that, he was about done.

Burn out. The words careened through his mind like breaking pool balls.

Problem was, he didn't have jack-shit outside of the Group. His parents were golfing their hearts out in a Florida retirement place. His brothers were all wrapped up in their wives and kids. Donovan had the job and a condo in Philly. Women came and went, unwilling to put up with his absences.

The cell buzzed, vibrating its way toward the puddle of condensation around his mug. Rossi again. No doubt shit was hitting the fan somewhere. "Donovan."

"I need you in New York. Yesterday."

"I'm on my way."

Jack pocketed his phone, then drained the rest of the gone-warm beer before throwing a handful of ones down next to the empty mug. "I'm sorry, Chris."

Time to chase the ghosts away.

The trip to the local clinic was mandatory, so Gallagher and Carmen were whisked straight there to suffer through being checked over and patched up. And, of course, because one of his injuries was a gunshot wound, the local law enforcement had to get the *don't ask* phone call.

But he'd managed to get them out of Arceneau's house and the White Mountains in one piece, so he didn't complain—too much—about the forced health care. In less than an hour he was cleared and went to the waiting room to see what was up.

Carmen hadn't come out yet, but Rossi and Grace were taking up a loveseat. As soon as they spotted him, they were on their feet. Rossi gave him a handshake and a look that said *I won't say it out loud but I love you, man, and I'm glad you're not dead* and he returned it with *I love you, too, man, and thanks for not giving up on us.* Then Grace gave him a quick, awkward hug.

"I didn't expect to see you, Grace."

She shrugged. "Danny's in Orlando with my parents. I was bored and you're practically in my backyard."

Rossi laughed. "And she kept Denton from killing me and dumping my body someplace even his best people couldn't find it."

They retook their places and Gallagher sat in the armchair across from them. "Did you figure out how they got to the helo yet?"

"They tagged the call number. They knew you were there the second you went for landing clearance. Arceneau must have had them watching for visits from certain people."

"Carmen found a record of transactions, which she'll hand over if she ever comes out. What the hell's taking them so long, anyway? She should be done by now."

Grace flashed him a knowing smile. "Five more minutes and then I'll go hunt her down."

He couldn't stop himself from glancing at the clock to mark the time. "We were almost clear when Carmen's gut told her to go back for the diary."

"You *thought* you were almost clear. They'd already gotten to the airport by then, and that helicopter was as good as down."

Gallagher shrugged, then gave them a verbal report of everything that happened between leaving New York and the ride to the hospital. Almost everything. He didn't mention the gum.

At four minutes and twenty seconds, Carmen walked into the waiting room. The greetings and hugs were repeated, but Carmen declined to sit.

She handed the pink diary to Rossi. "Gallagher can catch me up. I want to get out of here."

They all walked to the parking lot, Rossi talking the whole way. "Charlotte gave Grace your sizes, so you've each got a bag of clothes in the truck. You can drop us at the airport because we're heading back to New York, and then go on to the hotel. Charlotte sent you the info, and there's a drugstore next door where you can get anything else you need. Get a good night's sleep, then in the morning head to Manchester, leave the Hummer in parking and get your asses to New York."

"We could go with you now," Carmen said.

"I don't need you until tomorrow and you'll definitely want to be well-rested. Plus, the way you two smell, I'm not sharing a plane with you. No offense."

Chapter Six

Carmen was drying her twice-scrubbed skin with a soft hotel towel when she heard Gallagher's shower kick on in the room next door.

It was the perfect opportunity. She could get the man out of her system, yet the shower didn't imply the same intimacy as a bed. Get in, get some slick and soapy satisfaction, and get out.

Before she could talk herself out of it, she pulled on the supplied robe and slid her tool kit and two condoms into her pocket. The hotel locks were a joke and in less than a minute she was standing in Gallagher's room.

The clothes he'd been wearing were in a loose pile at the foot of the bed, as though he'd stepped out of them on his way to the shower. She dropped her robe beside them, palming the condoms. He'd left the bathroom door open and steam billowed out.

Good. She liked it hot.

Walking on silent bare feet into the bathroom, she admired his silhouette through the vinyl shower curtain. He was neither lean nor bulky, but perfectly honed muscle.

The question was, how safe did he feel? Gallagher wasn't a man to sneak up on. And yet, she couldn't resist. Could she take him?

She waited until he was facing the showerhead, his head tipped back to rinse the shampoo away. With her left hand she covered the last three rings on the bar to keep them silent and with her right she moved the curtain just enough to let her slide in without allowing more steam to escape.

She was still for a moment, pondering whether or not touching him from behind would get her knocked out before she could identify herself. If she waited until he turned around, he'd still be startled, but he might visually register her before swinging. She'd still win.

"You smell like peaches, babe."

Carmen laughed, even if she was a little irked he'd known she was there before she wanted him to. She took the soap from the shelf, leaving the condoms there, and started washing his back.

"I don't wear any scents when I'm working," she said. "Everything—soap, laundry detergent, shampoo—is unscented. During my down time I drown myself in the girly stuff. Bath oils and lotions and the whole nine yards."

His muscles twitched under her gliding fingertips. "I never knew that about you."

"That's because you've only known the unscented professional version. No flowery shit, though. I like fruit scents, mostly."

"Why did you buy peaches tonight?"

Carmen reached around to wash his chest, her breasts pressing against his soapy back. "Because when we were in the hospital after that mission to save Grace's son, they served peach cobbler."

"That's an interesting association," he said, and she slid her hands down his stomach to shut him up. It worked.

"You kept licking the peach juice off your lips and it made me ache watching you. So now the scent of peaches is all wrapped up in this Gallagher, tongue, sticky, aching kind of thing."

He turned in her arms. "That's my favorite kind of thing."

"But now I'll smell peaches and remember I couldn't even get the drop on you in the shower."

"You're even better than I thought, babe. If you'd gone unscented, you'd have had me." He grinned, a totally devastating grin that made her knees weak. "Not that I'll ever admit that again."

But he'd admitted it to her, and that was enough. Her hands slid over his body until she encountered a bandage. He'd taped plastic over the clean dressing, but she felt his abs tense when her fingers brushed the edge.

"Maybe we should reissue that rain check," she offered, even though the thought damn near killed her.

"No," he growled, backing her up against the cold tub surround. She hissed and arched away, but his body trapped her. "Remembering the night my balls exploded every time I smell peaches would suck. My mom bakes a lot of cobblers."

Carmen laughed, relaxing against the plastic already growing warm against her back. "Sitting around the family dinner table thinking about screwing me in the shower isn't much better."

"Babe, I've spent years thinking about making love to you."

There were those damn words again. *Making love.* The phrase should have sent her screaming, wet and naked, into the hall, but it didn't. She started to think about why, but then he kissed her and she didn't care anymore.

His breath was minty and the tang of his shaving cream

burned her nose. She tried to push away from the wall, to take control of the kiss, but he held her there while his tongue dipped into her mouth. It was no *getting to know each other* kiss like the ones they'd shared in the cabin.

This kiss was urgent, demanding. He threaded his fingers through her hair, his fingertips cradling her skull as she tipped her head back.

Gallagher caught her lip between his teeth and she sucked in a sharp breath. The muscles of his back twitched under her gliding fingertips and she hooked her leg around his, trying to pull him closer. He resisted for a second, and she was vaguely aware of the water shutting off.

Then he was pressed against her—warm and hard and slick. He lifted her until he could capture her nipple with his mouth and Carmen wrapped her legs around him as the gentle tugging pulled at every nerve ending in her body.

He supported her weight, his hands cupping her ass, while he took his time savoring first one breast and then the other, back and forth until she could only whimper and beat on his shoulder as her need reached critical mass.

Excruciatingly slowly, he lowered her, her aching center sliding down his flesh to rest against his erection. His mouth blazed a burning trail to her ear.

"Tell me what you like, babe," he told her, and the husky timbre of his voice sent a shiver through her. It would be so easy to surrender totally, to give too much of herself.

She swiped a condom from the shelf. "I like orgasms. Hard and fast ones. Immediate ones."

He only laughed and stepped out of the tub, still holding her. "I've been waiting years for this, babe. You aren't gettin' off that easy."

He dropped her on the end of the bed and plucked the foil

package out of her hand. "No pun intended."

Carmen found it damn hard to focus on his words when he was standing over her like some kind of sculpted and scarred warrior god. But even worse than the body was the look in his eyes.

There was some kind of...emotion there, and it scared the hell out of her. She didn't like emotion mixed with her sex. The few times she'd tried that hadn't worked out so well.

He crawled up over her, using his body to push her flat onto her back. Propping himself on one elbow, he pushed her wet hair off her face with his other hand and lowered his body onto hers.

His erection was thick and hard against her hipbone and she shifted so it rested against her lower abdomen. Unable to stop herself, despite the intimacy of the gesture, Carmen reached up and traced his mouth with the tip of a finger.

She'd known this man for nearly a decade, and she thought she'd seen him in every light. She'd even caught him staring at her with raw lust in his eyes when he thought she wasn't looking. But this Gallagher—with the emotion and the tenderness and the determination to savor this moment—she had no idea how to handle.

So she grabbed the condom he'd set beside her and rolled him onto his back. She straddled him and he reached up to cup her breasts in his hands, brushing his thumbs over her nipples. She started to tear open the wrapper, but he grinned and shook his head.

"Oh, yes," she said. "Right now."

In the blink of an eye she was flat on her back again, Gallagher straddling *her* and pinning her arms above her head with one hand. "Let it go, babe."

"Let *what* go?" she hissed, debating whether or not to try

for the headbutt.

"The power play. You're trying to control this and it's starting to piss me off."

"I like my sex fast and furious. You're taking the damn scenic route."

"With scenery like this?" He dipped his head to swipe his tongue over one taut nipple. "You bet."

Then he grinned down at her, naughty amusement lighting up the soft blue of his eyes, and she was lost. Resistance was futile and all that jazz. She'd go back to shoring up that emotional wall in the morning.

"Hey, you're shaking a little, babe," he said, loosening his hold on her wrists.

"I, uh...I've never done this with somebody like you."

"You've never had sex with an intelligent, good-looking, well-endowed, multi-talented guy?"

"No, I've never...forget it." She was trying to think of something flippant—something to goad him into getting on with it—when his lips touched hers again.

It was a soft kiss—a lover's kiss—and, as his hand slid down her stomach and between her legs to gently stroke her, Carmen felt more bricks in the wall crumbling.

"You've never let a man who cares for you more than you want to admit make love to you."

The seductive lull of his voice and the delicious friction of his fingers over her sensitive flesh must have weakened her because she made a sound he correctly took as agreement.

"It's better. Trust me," he said, and then he set out to prove it.

Carmen lost track of time as Gallagher explored her body with his hands and mouth, bringing her repeatedly to the brink of release, only to back her off. He teased her, stroked her, returning every few minutes to devour her mouth with his own.

"Gallagher," she gasped when she couldn't take anymore. "Now, dammit."

"John," he told her, and the crinkle of foil in his hand almost made her weep in anticipation of relief.

Seconds later he settled himself between her thighs and she lifted her hips as he *finally* entered her. He plunged his hands into her hair, his gaze holding hers as he filled her, withdrew almost all the way, then filled her again.

"Years," he whispered, "and it's even sweeter than I imagined."

It was, and she raked her nails down his back to his ass, urging him to thrust faster. He ignored her, building the tension with slow, lazy strokes.

"Please," she begged, pride thrown away in the face of her body's need.

His mouth turned up a little at the corners, but the beads of sweat across his forehead and the trembling of his shoulders gave him away. He was as far out on the ragged edge as she was.

"God, you feel so good, babe." His pace quickened and Carmen moaned deep in her throat. "Look at me, Carmen, and let it come."

So close. "I feel like I'm going to fall. Freefalling, with no ropes. No net."

"I'll catch you." His hands fisted in her hair and he seared her mouth with a brutal kiss as he thrust deeper, faster. "I'll always catch you."

"Please...John..."

With a growl he lifted her ankles to his shoulders and drove into her. Carmen's mind exploded with sensation as the orgasm wracked her body.

He groaned her name as he climaxed, and when he let her legs drop and collapsed on top of her, she wrapped her arms around him.

Slowly their breathing returned to normal, and she felt his pulse slow under the palm of her hand. A strange sense of disappointment pinged her when he slid free and rolled to dispose of the condom.

She wasn't ready to get up and go back to her room yet. She should, though, just to reestablish some distance between them.

But then he was hauling her back into his embrace, one of his legs hooking over hers. He nuzzled her hair and then, a minute later, he was snoring.

Carmen told herself it would be rude to wake him after all he'd gone through for her. She told herself, since they weren't officially back on the clock yet, it was really no different from the nights in the cabin.

Tomorrow would be soon enough to deal with the fallout.

She didn't allow herself to dwell on the fact there was no place she'd rather be at that moment than in his arms. But she did turn her head and press a soft kiss to his chest before she closed her eyes and followed him into sleep.

Five more minutes. Carmen pulled the blanket over her head and snuggled closer to Gallagher.

"Four scrambled eggs," he muttered against the back of her head. "Wheat toast. Bacon. Extra sausage. A short stack of pancakes. Coffee. Orange juice. More coffee."

"We having company for breakfast?"

"That's for me. I'll order you something, too."

She laughed and kicked backwards with her heel, catching his shin. "No room service."

"What? Hell, I should give Charlotte a roll of paper towels as a wedding gift."

"This isn't the big city, but there's a diner down the street."

"I wonder if they'll deliver."

"Mmm...probably not. Besides we have to get to New York, so no hanging around in bed all day."

He hooked his arm over her, trapping her against him. "I don't want to go yet."

Neither did she, which was the best reason to get up and go.

She liked waking up in Gallagher's arms. She liked lying in bed talking about breakfast like normal people. And she'd liked the feel of him inside her—the look in his eyes as he took her—*way* too much.

It was almost too easy to imagine doing it again...and again. Making love, sleeping in his arms, waking up there. Then going to work.

Never last, she reminded herself. They were too different, wanted different things in life and that was why everything from chewing his gum to last night had been one giant screw-up.

"Dibs on the shower," she said with forced cheerfulness, throwing back the covers.

He reached for her, but she evaded his grasp and grabbed her bathrobe. And, while she knew it wouldn't keep him out if he wanted in, she locked the bathroom door.

It was the right thing to do, she knew. Once they were back in New York—back on the job—the last couple of days would fade to nothing more than a fond memory and things would return to normal.

A few tears escaped to run down her cheeks and she turned her face into the spray to wash them away.

It *was* the right thing to do. She was almost sure of it.

When the bathroom doorknob didn't turn in his hand, Gallagher knew it was over.

He'd been expecting this. Even as they made love, she'd tried to hold herself back. But he hadn't expected it to be so soon. At least not until they'd reached New York.

For a long moment he stood with his hand on the cheap metal doorknob, staring at the flimsy luan door. He could be in there in a second. He could bust in there and shake her—make her tell him *why*.

Why couldn't she give them a chance. Why she could trust him with her life, but not her heart. Why she was so strong and fearless in the face of danger but ran from him.

Instead he pulled on the clothes Charlotte had provided, the cargo pants and T-shirt identical to the ones he'd taken off, only newer and scratchier—then checked his weapon.

He made the bed because his mother would somehow know if he didn't, even a hotel bed, then set his pack by the door.

When Carmen stepped out of the bathroom, the belt on her robe knotted tightly, she scanned the room. "I'll head back to my room and grab my stuff. Meet you out front in ten minutes."

Then she was gone and he was left staring at the door.

It wasn't quite as over as she thought, he told himself. They'd head in and deal with whatever Rossi had going on. But when the job was over, he was going to do some good, old-fashioned courting.

Okay, not too old-fashioned, since he hoped a lot of the courting would take place naked. It was time to step it up a notch.

But it was going to be a long, awkward trip back to New York.

Chapter Seven

Jack Donovan was surprised to see Gallagher and Carmen at the conference table. He'd been filled in on their near-death, near-sodium overdose experience, but they looked to be in fighting shape.

Both a little tense, he noted. Jaws and shoulders tight, with zero eye contact between the two. Interesting.

"Here's the deal," Rossi said, and Donovan pulled up a chair next to Connor O'Brien and gave the boss his full attention. "Arceneau will give full cooperation to both governments, including dropping a dime on some as-yet-unidentified co-conspirators in exchange for a favor."

The agents all made dismissive sounds, Jack included, but it was Carmen who spoke. "The book will hang him. We don't need to do him any favors."

"ID-ing some of his fellow scumbags would be nice," Gallagher pointed out.

"Then, there's this," Rossi said, and he turned his computer screen so they could see it.

A picture of a beautiful young woman. Long, blonde hair, pretty blue eyes and a perfect pageant smile. She looked like she could be Miss Name the Crop at any small town fair in the Midwest.

"Isabelle Arceneau," Rossi continued. "Daughter of Jean Arceneau, currently twenty-three, and previously believed to be doing post-graduate work somewhere in Europe. That was not the case."

Unrest rippled through the room as the four agents got a clue as to where he was heading. Jack stared at the picture. At her eyes, specifically. Isabelle had pale blue irises ringed by a darker shade of blue, and they damn near sparkled with confidence and humor as she smiled at the camera. Or whoever was behind it. It was a casual shot, a candid, and she was fond of the photographer.

"In June of '06, Arceneau and his daughter were part of an international media op highlighting the situation in Matunisia. They went off the grid for half a day, after which Arceneau gave the explanation Isabelle had gotten scared and gone on to Europe early to meet with some friends.

"That was a lie. Le Roux got her. If Arceneau performed every task given him for five years, he'd get his daughter back. If he refused or was apprehended, Isabelle would be made to suffer until she died."

Almost two years those animals had had her?

A stab of grief took him by surprise. That girl—the one in the picture—was gone. Even if Isabelle Arceneau was still alive, she'd never be that girl again.

She was already a ghost.

Maybe he was a little soft after yesterday's beer because his hands curled into fists and he had to clear his throat.

It wasn't goddamn fair that her life was ruined. For what?

"Five years is smart," Gallagher said. "Less time and you can't establish the system to get anything done. More time and the parent thinks it's worth the risk of going to the authorities. Five years is hard but, when dealing with people like Le Roux, must seem like the lesser of some really bad evils."

Jack couldn't look away from the photo. "How long until Le Roux knows we fucked over Arceneau's operation?"

"They already know," Rossi said. "They had a guy with Arceneau. And there was a transaction in the works we interrupted, shorting Le Roux six-point-five mil."

He pushed a few buttons on the keyboard and the photo of Isabelle disappeared. "Every two weeks, Arceneau would receive a web-cam video from the compound, letting him know Isabelle was alive and serving as a reminder of what was at stake."

He clicked play and Isabelle's face once again filled the screen. Only this time it was video and the pageant perfection was gone. "This was sent to him last night, shortly before he contacted us."

Isabelle Arceneau was filthy and bruised, with blood oozing from a cut on her lip. But even though tears filled her eyes, there was a strength there Jack couldn't miss.

She *was* still alive—that girl from the photo—and hanging on by the no doubt ragged tips of her fingernails. This one wouldn't quit.

When she forced her lips into a trembling but brave smile, Jack felt it beating back the dark clouds hovering over him. It was innocents like her that made his job—and therefore his whole freakin' life—worth a damn. He could save her.

Isabelle Arceneau was strong enough to hold on. She just needed somebody who wouldn't let go.

"Papa," she said to the camera in English, with only a hint of French accent, "they're going to kill me soon. He said to tell you if you got them the money you owe them, I won't suffer."

"Give the money to the orphans, Papa." She was talking faster and Jack leaned further over the table, trying to hear.

"I'm going to die anyway and I don't want—"

She was jerked away from the webcam, the way her neck snapped back letting Jack deduce some asshole had yanked her by the hair. There was the unmistakable sound of flesh striking flesh and then the transmission ended.

"I think we should go," he said, and they all turned to look at him.

"It's fucking Matunisia, man," Gallagher said. "Only the homicidal and the suicidal go there."

Or guys with nothing to lose. "I'm in. Tell the Feds you'll send me and if I get her out, there's a deal. If I can't...it was worth a shot."

"She might already be dead," Rossi pointed out.

God, he hoped not. He needed something to hold on to. Something to believe in. And he believed Isabelle Arceneau was strong enough to survive. He believed he could bring her home. "But she might be alive."

Gallagher liked to play Joe Hero as much as the next guy, but he was leaning toward a regretful but necessary pass on this job. Sending somebody into Matunisia for one person? Even with the added bonus of busting a few other launderers and go-betweens, it wasn't a good deal.

Especially for the guys expected to take on one of the most brutal and savage terrorist regimes on the planet.

"Could it be done?" Rossi asked, and he didn't have to look up to know he was asking him. Mission planning was Gallagher's job.

"No."

"Yes," Donovan said at the same time, and Gallagher wondered where the guy's head was. Isabelle Arceneau was pretty, but she was a little young for him and more than likely already dead.

"I'm not following your dick to my death, and neither are they," Gallagher said in a low voice. "Let's just put that on the table right now."

The other agent tried to stare him down, but Gallagher didn't even blink. He knew if he didn't give thumbs up, Rossi and the Group would walk away.

"She deserves a chance," Donovan finally said. "She's willing to suffer to keep that money out of Le Roux's pockets."

"Isabelle Arceneau won't be the only one," Carmen pointed out. "If that's his M.O., there will be other loved ones being held in the compound and we can't save them all."

"But we can save *her.*"

"No, we can't," she said in a more gentle voice than Gallagher had ever heard her use. She didn't think they could do it, either.

Meanwhile, he was also keenly aware of Rossi's stare boring into the side of head, as if he could get the wheels in Gallagher's mind turning by force of will.

And, against his better judgment, they did.

Common sense aside, it was damn hard to turn away from a hurting, innocent girl. On a mission, people lived and people died. It was a fact of life every person at the table was well-versed in. Even looking at that girl and knowing her survival rested on his shoulders shouldn't be a strange new burden for him.

But that was in action. To sit in a boardroom and coldly determine her fate—if he said yes, she had a chance, no matter how slim, and if he said no she was dead—was soul crushing.

It was a sucker's bet, but he looked at Donovan. "Your

cover as an arms dealer ever get blown?"

That got everybody's attention. "No, it's intact. Every so often Charlotte feeds some bullshit through cyber-channels, keeping Hans Koenig on the radar."

"Then there's a very, very slim chance we can get her out, but you're going to have to throw yourself down in front of the bus to do it."

The other agent didn't even blink. "I don't care if it runs my ass over as long as it slows down enough for Isabelle Arceneau to jump on and get a ride out. I'm in, all the way."

"I'm not assigning anybody on this one," Rossi said. "And I won't hold it against anybody who opts out. Strictly voluntary, every step of the way."

"I'm in," O'Brien said immediately, which didn't come as a surprise. He didn't have a wife or kids, and he and Donovan partnered in the field more often than not.

"My wife's head would explode if I tried to breach the compound, but I'll go along as in-country support," Rossi offered. He was still recovering from a bombing of the Group's headquarters and he was about ninety-seven percent. Three percent shy of taking on Le Roux head to head. "Can't let you guys have *all* the fun."

"I'm in," Carmen said, and Gallagher's heart seized up in his chest like a blown engine.

When he'd said "*we* can get her out", he'd meant him and Donovan. O'Brien. Maybe Rossi. Not in a million freakin' years was Carmen part of that we.

"Matunisia's no place for a woman," he said with all the authority he could muster, praying she'd listen.

How could a look freeze and incinerate at the same time? She managed it. "It's no place for *anybody*."

She wasn't the only one staring at him. Everybody else in the room was waiting for his response, too.

Too bad he didn't have one. There were good reasons for her to be a part of the team. For one, she was sneaky as hell and, dressed in traditional Matunisian peasant garb with the head covering, she'd attract a lot less attention than the guys.

But, dammit, he didn't want her in the line of fire. And taking her into a country where the rats had more rights than the women?

"I'm a member of this Group, Gallagher," she said, clearly sick of waiting. "You need to respect me as a professional, or you—"

"I do." He cut her off and decided to lay his cards on the table. A situation like Matunisia required full disclosure. "I'm worried about my own ability to focus with you out there."

If there'd been a cricket in the room, he'd have had center stage for a good thirty or forty seconds.

"Get over it or take yourself off the team," she snapped. "I'm in."

He should have kept his mouth shut. He could have stuck with his original answer—rescuing Isabelle Arceneau was impossible.

But he couldn't tell Rossi to clear her image off the screen and then go home and forget about her. Couldn't sleep at night. That and he had a hunch Donovan was going with or without the Group. Losing him would be a blow to all of them.

But losing Carmen...

He could make Rossi cut her out. There were solid reasons for not taking a female along, and he knew he could convince the others it was a bad idea. Bottom line, they couldn't do this without him.

When he made eye contact with her, her dark eyes told him two things. One, she expected him to say no. And two, when he did, he'd lose her anyway.

Gallagher leaned back in his chair and folded his arms. "Listen up, boys—and girl—because this is the plan."

Phase one went more or less smoothly, much to Gallagher's surprise. He really didn't have a good feeling about this job.

The Devlin Group—minus Jack Donovan—arrived in Barasa, Matunisia's provisional capital city, on a typical day for the region. Hot, humid and as pungent as a horse's ass.

Being a fan of tropical climates was one thing. Scratching his scalp while making his way through a cesspool of humanity was another thing entirely. It was only a five-minute walk from the helicopter they'd parked at the half-ass airport—the Group's private Bombardier jet being a little too conspicuous—to the hotel, which was why they'd chosen lodging in the crappier part of the city. Less than a two-minute run if need be.

Gallagher took in as many details of the area as possible, all with a goofy "dude, check this out" look plastered on his face. Didn't want to look like he was casing the joint.

They'd arrived under the guise of being humanitarian filmmakers making a documentary on the atrocities being perpetrated on the country by guerilla regimes.

Kissing the provisional government's ass, along with a hefty dollop of monetary lubrication, had not only gotten them in the country within twenty-four hours, but had gotten their "camera equipment" bags in, as well.

Now the true vigilance had to kick in. Nobody—whether they claimed to be with the provisional government or not—

could be trusted. And Gallagher, Rossi and O'Brien all in one spot looked like exactly what they were—a group of guys ready to kick the shit out of any takers.

Since Rossi would, if all went well, spend the entire mission in and around the Hotel Jardin, he got to wear the padding. Just a little strategic lining here and there to disguise the muscle definition and make him look like a guy who'd made a few too many trips to the buffet line in a country where the food was actually edible.

O'Brien was nominated as the geek. Non-prescription black-rimmed glasses, a T-shirt with some nonsense equation emblazoned on the front. Ridiculous shorts. He wore a soft elastic brace designed to encourage him to slouch a little, and an oddly-shaped insert in one shoe to keep him from swaggering.

Carmen had her hair in two braids down the side of her face, a pink ball cap on backwards and, with pink tennis shoes on her feet and a T-shirt preaching environmental responsibility, she looked about fifteen.

Gallagher went with his traditional loud-as-hell Hawaiian shirt and didn't wash his hair. Distracting details were key. Anything to keep people from looking too closely at their faces— into their eyes. You couldn't disguise the look in a person's eye.

When the door of their two room, so-called suite was closed and locked, every one of them grabbed a bottled water and collapsed with relief. It was draining, being aware not only of what everybody around you was doing, but being conscious of your own body language and the vibe you were putting out there.

"You're absolutely sure Donovan's cover checks out?" Rossi asked him for the thousandth time.

"It's clean. As long as Le Roux doesn't have rat-sniffing

superpowers, getting in should be a piece of cake."

It was the getting out—with a traumatized female package—that had Gallagher rummaging through his pack for the ibuprofen.

The set-up was simple on the surface—Arceneau was released due to a lack of strong evidence, but his finances were under the microscope. He couldn't get the 6.5 million to Le Roux, but he could substitute an equivalent amount of American and Russian arms. He knew a highly-recommended guy willing to provide the arms with Arceneau's holdings as collateral for future payment when he was cleared.

Le Roux, knowing he wasn't going to get his money, but smart enough to walk away with more than a dead girl, had agreed almost immediately that Hans Koenig could enter the compound. The Group was in the air an hour later.

Now they were in the hotel, unpacking gear, setting up the computers and the communication system. Or rather, Gallagher was working on setting things up while O'Brien rummaged through the oversized bag Gallagher had brought.

"Jesus, G, is there a kitchen sink at the bottom of this?"

"Flunked out of the Boy Scouts, but the *Be Prepared* stuck with me."

O'Brien held up the harness of a rapid extraction method developed in the Fifties. "Kickin' it old school?"

"Oldie but goodie, dude. It's my good luck charm for jungle jobs."

"You ever had to use it?"

"No, that's why it's good luck."

"I hope it works, man, because if ever we needed luck..."

Chapter Eight

There was nothing like walking totally alone into the compound of one of the most brutal regimes in history to get the old adrenaline pumping.

As the front gate opened, Jack Donovan calculated less than two minutes remained until he knew which way it was going to go. One, he'd be admitted and they'd start negotiations. Two, Le Roux was smarter than he was greedy and Jack would be tortured, skinned and tossed in the body pile.

He lost count of the guns pointed at him, but took special note of the one poking him in the chest. "You have weapons?" the guy attached to the trigger finger asked.

That was kind of like asking a Rolex dealer if he had the time, so he gave the thug a scornful look. "Of course."

A flurry of hands relieved him of both guns, the knife and his phone in a matter of seconds. They rifled through his briefcase, then declared him clean. Thankfully they'd never seen James Bond or Mission Impossible because they left him his watch. Maybe they didn't have cable.

His focus snapped back with a vengeance when the crowd parted for the man whose real name nobody even remembered—Le Roux.

He wasn't a big guy. A little on the short side, and wiry. Sporting the full camo favored by the international killer warlord set. Skin, eyes and hair like the darkest mahogany.

They, whoever they were, had begun calling him Le Roux—
the redhead—when he was still in his teens. A foot soldier in
the first of several regimes to terrorize Matunisia, he'd taken
part in the well-organized massacre of four key villages. That
was the first time he'd painted his hair red with the blood of
innocent victims. It wasn't the last.

While his hair was clot-free at the moment, Jack had heard
the man grew more vicious and batshit crazy with every body
he'd stepped on to get where he was. He could see it now in the
man's eyes.

Le Roux's nostrils flared and Jack got the impression he
was sniffing. What, exactly, did a Matunisian pseudo-general
expect a German arms dealer to smell like?

"You come alone? Very strange for a rich man."

"I'm the only person I trust."

His answer and eau d'international flight must have passed
muster because Le Roux gestured and Jack was handed his
briefcase before being herded into the largest building in the
compound. It was a big common room, dominated by a massive
table and a map of Matunisia.

Unfortunately, as the thugs spread out, straddling chairs
or holding up walls, they didn't put their guns down. They
simply holstered them, swung them back on their straps, or set
them on their laps. This wasn't a bunch likely to let down their
guard.

"You come, show me this list," Le Roux ordered, gesturing
toward a chair at the big table.

Jack withdrew the catalog of doom from his briefcase but
he didn't toss it onto the table, nor did he sit. It was time to
play ball. "I want to see the girl first."

Le Roux hesitated and Jack forced himself to keep his face a blank slate. Was she already dead?

"Why?"

"If she's dead, Arceneau's not going to pay me, and I don't want to have to kill him. It's bad for my reputation when my associates turn up missing."

Everything hinged on how badly Le Roux wanted the guns. Because he had no hostage with which to control the arms dealer, he'd have to let him walk out unharmed in order to get them. But Jack had to be careful how hard he pushed because the terrorist's volatile temper wasn't exactly a secret.

Finally the man made a gesture to one of his men and three minutes later Isabelle Arceneau was shoved into the room so hard she landed sprawled at Donovan's feet.

Forcing dispassion into every part of his face and body, he stared down at the young woman. She was bruised, bloody, her clothes in tatters. And her hair...

Her long blonde hair was gone. All that remained was a too-short frizzy cloud around her head, and the ends appeared to have been singed.

"What happened to her hair?"

Le Roux shrugged. "Kitchen accident. The fire or something. *Get up.*"

Isabelle pushed herself to her knees, and then painfully made it to her feet, but she kept her eyes on Jack's feet.

He made a sound of disgust. "She was more attractive in the photograph Arceneau showed me. I intended to use her to make this worth my while. Interest, if you will, while I wait for my payment."

The list of weapons available must have caught Le Roux's attention, because he didn't waste any time shoving her at

Jack. "The parts of her you want are still attractive enough, my friend. And the tits on this one make up for the ugly hair, yes?"

He reached out and ripped Isabelle's top away, but she barely flinched. And, though it turned Jack's stomach, he had no choice but to look. Young and firm breasts, a little on the smaller side, but it was the bruises that drew his eye. Bruises up and down her arms, across the top of her shoulder. Two larger ones on her abdomen, one bearing the faint shadowing of boot tread, made him sick.

"She's part of the package," Jack said, and it definitely wasn't a question.

"The bitch isn't leaving here until I get my money or my guns, but you can use her while you're here."

Jack nodded. "I'll get my money's worth from this one."

He hadn't believed for a minute Le Roux was just going to let Isabelle leave with him, but at least she was relatively unharmed and he'd have access to her.

For now it would have to be enough.

The Group had audio from Donovan through his watch. It was risky, but Charlotte had hooked them up with some top-notch components even Gallagher had trouble spotting.

Major drawback—it was one-way comm. They couldn't communicate with Donovan short of standing outside the compound gate with a bullhorn.

O'Brien did most of the listening. He was Donovan's primary partner and he knew him better than anyone. If Donovan tried to give them anything, O'Brien would be the one to catch it.

Carmen had spent some time dropping American dollars at

the bakery, apparently a hotbed of female gossip, where she'd learned an unpleasant fact from a couple of women who'd been favored whores until they hit their twenties. Le Roux's men never put their guns down. They drank, ate and picked their noses left-handed if need be and, since it was unlikely the entire army consisted of natural southpaws, that spoke of discipline and training.

"He's not going to get out of there easily," Rossi said. The men were going over what they had while Carmen was out interviewing women who'd worked in the compound for their imaginary documentary.

Every second she was gone took another minute off Gallagher's life.

He stopped looking over O'Brien's shoulder and pulled up some couch. "We knew going in getting him out was going to be a crap shoot."

They both stared at the aerial satellite shots spread over the coffee table. As Jack's casual comments to the guerillas during a tour of the camp fed them tidbits of info, they were marking the photos they'd scrounged from old US intelligence reports, but a viable weakness had yet to pop out at them. Bad idea trusting outdated intelligence, too, but it was all they had.

Gallagher shifted some of the photos around, leaning over the coffee table to get a closer look. It was frustrating as hell to be coming up with a plan *after* sending a guy in, but they'd had no choice. They had to get the offer on the table and Donovan inside before Le Roux killed the girl.

"If we could get a couple of masks to them, we could gas the camp. Just put everybody to sleep for a while."

Rossi shook his head. "Too many innocents. Not safe for the very young or very old. I'd rather this go down clean. But we can't trust Le Roux to hand over the girl even if we gave up the weapons."

Which was something they wouldn't consider. Even though the Group could get its hands on anything, they couldn't swap an arsenal capable of taking thousands of lives for one life. If Donovan couldn't talk Isabelle out of there and he refused to leave without her, they'd have to get them out.

So far they hadn't even come up with a Plan A.

"That small cliff behind the compound might work," Gallagher said. "If I conceal a rope and gear in the crevice and create a hellacious diversion around the front, he could help her climb out. He's a hell of a climber."

"Was."

Something in Rossi's voice made Gallagher look over. "What do you mean?"

"I'm not comfortable sharing this, but since it might affect the job—Donovan hasn't climbed in three years. There was an accident and his friend's gear failed. Donovan couldn't hold him."

"Shit." He turned back to the photos, sifting through scenarios in his head. "He might have to choose between his fear and the girl."

"He hasn't managed an ascent since. He could freeze halfway up and they both die."

"This was never a job with a guaranteed happily ever after, dude. He knew going in the odds sucked and any chance is better than no chance."

There was a knock on the door—the opening bar of *The Addams Family* theme song—and Carmen slid in. She was dressed in colorful native garb, her hair hidden under a turban. While her Latina skin wasn't nearly dark enough, with a scarf she passed for interracial if nobody looked too hard. The women she'd been talking to thought she was an American trying to respect their customs. Everybody else, they were hoping, wouldn't look twice.

"I can't get in," she told them as she peeled off layers of garments. "Well, I can get in, but not legitimately. Laundry women, cooks, whores, you name it. All personally vetted by Le Roux or one of his so-called lieutenants. And, God, could it be any hotter out there?"

"Smoke bombs and a small chopper?" Rossi offered.

Gallagher shook his head. "Rocket launchers in a wide perimeter. Only his helicopter flies over the camp. Le Roux was close enough to the watch we could hear him brag about it. Donovan must have scratched his head or something so we could eavesdrop."

Down to a tank top and spandex shorts, Carmen grabbed a bottle of water and sat on the other end of the couch. "Can Jack hijack it? Fly themselves out?"

He tried like hell not to be distracted by the tangy scent of her overheated body. "No. We can't take the chance he has it rigged for a remote detonation in that situation. Le Roux might be jungle raised, but money and brute force have bought him association with some pretty savvy people."

"I found out something interesting from a cleaning lady," Carmen said. "It seems the provisional government has a spy in Le Roux's camp. Whenever he can he sends info back, which is kept in a file in the Ministry building. A guy by the name of Keita manages him."

"No shit." Gallagher nodded. "We need that file."

"They won't let us see it," Rossi told him. "They took the bribe to look the other way on our luggage, but this is a whole new level. There's been an abatement of hostilities and they don't want *anybody* pissing him off. They also won't want to risk their guy being exposed."

"Then we take it," Carmen said.

Gallagher snorted. "There are people in that building around the clock, and it's their primary government building."

Carmen smiled and looked at him, a challenge in her dark eyes. "Guess it's a good thing you brought me after all, huh?"

"Four hours of surveillance isn't enough."

Carmen blew out an aggravated breath and scooted back away from the edge of the roof on her stomach. "Ticking clock and we don't know how many ticks we have. We have to do it tonight and it'll be dawn in a couple of hours."

"It's stupid to rush it," he argued as he followed, keeping his head down as two men passed below them on the street.

She didn't bother responding this time. She could have schematics and a S.W.A.T. escort and Gallagher would still bitch like an overprotective mother.

There was a difference between rushing a job and abbreviating the timeline.

Shortly before public hours ended, she, Gallagher and Rossi had entered the ministry building under the guise of wanting to interview government officials for their documentary. They hadn't expected to get beyond reception, but they'd managed to establish there was no security panel inside the door, nor any sign of security cameras. If they had them, they'd have them in the lobby.

"We're supposed to interview a Mr. Keita," Rossi had told the receptionist, who had a less than stellar mastery of English. "We can just go on back. He's on the second floor, right?"

"No. Floor three. But he's...gone now. Tomorrow. We

closing now."

They'd made a small show of being put out, but left before they upset her enough to make her nervous.

Now she had a vague destination—the third floor—which was dark. The rich and powerful top-floor denizens apparently got to work normal hours. The first two floors spilled light from several of the windows she could see.

And wonder of all wonders, the ministry building had a fire escape, right there in the back, hidden in the shadows cast by surrounding buildings.

"In about three minutes that guy's going to come out for a smoke break," she told him. "As soon as he goes in, I am, too."

"I'll be here. And if you have any trouble at all, I'll be wherever you are in thirty seconds flat." She went back down the tree that had given them access to the neighboring roof, leaving them to communicate through the comm.

"If I need you, I'll let you know." The back door of the ministry building opened and there was a clunk as the smoker propped it with a cinder block.

"This time if I tell you to get out, you get the hell out," Gallagher said, and then the almost imperceptible beep told her his handheld had synced with hers so he could monitor her location. "You didn't listen to me in Canada and look what happened."

"If I'd listened to you, we wouldn't have found the diary and Arceneau probably wouldn't have turned himself in. You do your job and let me do mine."

The silence was crushing as they waited for the smoker to stub out his butt and head back inside. When the door clanged shut behind him, Carmen went. She crossed to the fire escape and, situating herself as close to the brick wall as possible, began to climb. She moved carefully, with slow movements that shouldn't attract attention.

When she reached the third floor window, she slid her hand into a pocket of the jumpsuit and pulled out a small can of WD-40, which she squirted down into the window runners. Then she went to work on the screen. Her favorite tool, a virtually silent mini-drill with a Phillips bit took care of the screws and she laid the entire panel flat on the platform of the fire escape. If the smoker happened to look up during his next nicotine fix, he shouldn't notice anything amiss.

She'd been hoping they'd be careless about a third-floor window, but when she tried to push up on the sash, she met resistance. "Shit."

"What's wrong?" Gallagher pounced on her word before she'd finished getting it out of her mouth.

"Nothing. It's locked, that's all."

"Can you get by it?"

"Of course." It would be faster to cut the pane, but it was important the government officials have no idea their offices had been breached. With any luck they wouldn't know the file was missing until the Group had left Matunisia and it was delivered by courier to the receptionist.

Precious seconds became minutes as she worked at the pivoting lock with a hook and thin, alloy straightedge. Finally the lock disengaged and she slid the slash up. Thanks to the lubricant, it slid almost silently and, after climbing into the office, she lowered it behind her.

"I'm in." She gave her eyes a few seconds to adjust to the dark interior. When at all possible she avoided wearing night-vision gear. It not only screwed with her depth perception and peripheral vision, but she'd be at a serious, painful disadvantage should somebody flip a light on.

An ancient metal desk took up a quarter of the room and

she went to it. She pressed her thumb and forefinger together to turn on the LED light in the tip of her glove. The mail on the desk wasn't addressed to Keita.

Sticking close to the walls, where the old wooden floors were less likely to squeak, she made her way into the hall. For once Lady Luck was on her side. Cheap metal name plaques hung outside every office.

She was halfway down the hall when the overhead lights came on and heavy footsteps clunked on the stairs.

Chapter Nine

"Carmen, the lights are on."

No shit, Sherlock. She didn't say it aloud, though, because she was too busy moving.

The closest office wasn't Keita's, but she ducked into it, automatically stepping to the right. Just in case whoever was coming belonged to her current location, she slid between the open door and the wall.

"Situation?" Gallagher barked into her earpiece.

She didn't dare answer him with those heavy footsteps coming down the hall. But if she didn't give him something, he was liable to come bursting through the front door and up the stairs, guns blazing. She reached up and tapped her mic twice to acknowledge she'd heard him, while pulling her Taser from its sheath.

Using it would be almost worst case scenario. Rossi had practically run out of oxygen stressing over and over how important it was to leave no trace of their trespassing and it was hard to hide jolting a guy senseless.

As the footsteps continued past her current hiding place, Carmen slid out from behind the door and risked a peek down the hall. Dammit, the guy had a briefcase. Who the hell went to work at four in the morning?

The man turned into an office and flicked his light on. And there, two doors past his, she saw the nameplate for Keita. Of course.

But, at the end of the hallway was a coffee station. The way she saw it, Mr. Early Bird was going to drop his stuff in his office, then get the caffeine brewing.

Without second-guessing herself, Carmen darted across the hall into the darkened office next to his, then waited. The next step would be a little riskier, considering the wattage those bare bulbs were putting out there, but she wasn't going through this again the following night.

After a few moments of shuffling around, she heard him go into the hallway and she stepped out, too. He was heading for the coffee machine and she fell in behind him, close enough to give him a hit with the Taser if need be, but not close enough to disturb that hair-prickling, personal space zone. She kept her gaze over his shoulder, not staring directly at him and prayed the floor wouldn't squeak.

When they reached Keita's office, she let Mr. Early Bird pull away slightly, then shifted into the darkened room. The footsteps stopped as she once again tucked herself between the open door and the wall.

She heard his shoes slide on the wood as he turned, probably wondering if he'd seen movement or if his still caffeine-deprived mind was playing tricks on him.

Keita's light flipped on and Carmen froze, breathing slowly and silently as seconds tipped by. Then Mr. Early Bird insulted his silliness in French, chuckled and shut the light off.

She waited while he set up the coffee machine and then waited some more while it brewed, the aroma wafting through the offices and making her mouth water. Finally, after she twice had to tap on her mic to silence Gallagher's demands for an update, Mr. Early Bird shuffled back to his office with his coffee.

It took her less than a minute to pick the lock on Keita's filing cabinet and then almost as long to open the first drawer. She didn't want to risk the WD-40 with the documents, but based on the condition of everything else, she was afraid the drawers would squeal.

An additional two minutes to locate the file. After scanning the disappointingly few documents it contained, she slid it into her jumpsuit and closed and relocked the drawer.

Unfortunately now she had to get past Mr. Early Bird's office while praying there weren't any more overachievers about to descend on the building. She had no choice but to go back out the window she'd come in. Not only was the fire escape there, but she had to replace the screen to cover her tracks.

Shit.

Poking her head into the hall, Carmen checked out the coffee machine, noting the location of the paper towels and the fact the machine was fed from piping, rather than needing a reservoir filled. Staying close to the wall, she went to the station and hit the brew button. Then she ducked into an office across the hall, but still out of view of the lit office.

It didn't take very long for the additional coffee to spill out of the already almost full pot Mr. Early Bird had just brewed. The sizzling and spitting drew his attention and he swore as he stepped into the hall. As he fumbled with one hand, taking the full pot out and trying to keep up with the steady drip by putting a mug on the hotplate, and grabbing at paper towels with the other, Carmen backed slowly down the hallway until she reached her point of entry.

"Exit clear?" she asked Gallagher in an almost non-existent voice.

"Clear."

She slid the sash open and stepped onto the fire escape, then closed it behind her. Within seconds she'd reattached the screen and made her way down the fire escape. When she reached the bottom she caught the bundle Gallagher dropped from the roof and wrapped herself in the bright, oversized scarves favored by the local women.

"Meet you back there," she said as she walked down the alley toward the hotel.

It took Donovan almost an hour to determine the small *guest* hut he'd been given was clean. If he'd had a sweeper it would have taken two minutes, but there hadn't been any way to smuggle one in. After examining every crack, crevice and surface of the room, he was confident the only people who could hear him were the crew back in the hotel.

During the entire search, Isabelle Arceneau—wearing his spare shirt—sat on the edge of the bed, looking down at the floor. He'd noticed right off she didn't make eye contact. Ever, with anybody.

"What happened to your hair?" he asked, keeping his tone light and hopefully reassuring.

She still wouldn't look at him. "A kitchen accident. I got too close to the fire."

"Bullshit. Hair doesn't burn uniformly around your head like that."

Her gaze did lift to his face then, but skittered away. "It *did* burn."

"They yank you around by your hair? Control you with it?" He'd seen it himself on the video they'd sent her father.

Her throat worked before she nodded. "I'm not allowed to

have knives or scissors. I used a stick I kept heating in a candle flame."

"Must have taken a long time. And it was a big risk, making these people unhappy. What they've done to you is tame compared to what they're capable of."

"I...I know." And he could see she did by the shudder that rippled through her. "It was worth the risk. It probably sounds stupid to you, but..."

When she didn't finish, he did it for her. "It was one thing you could control."

She nodded, and Jack almost smiled, until he noticed the trembling. He could almost imagine her panicking on the inside. Had she told him too much? Would he use her confession to hurt her? When he reached out a hand, intending to give her a comforting touch, she flinched.

Dammit. There were two ways to play his hand, and he was almost to the point of flipping a coin. He could stay in character, even with Isabelle, which was definitely the safest way to play it without having judged the girl's acting skills. Expecting a traumatized young woman to keep the secret of his identity was risky.

But Hans Koenig, the German arms dealer, would take her to bed and use her until he handed her over to her father, just as he'd told Le Roux. There was no way in hell he'd rape this girl. Even to save her life.

Telling her who he really was, though, was very risky. One slip of the tongue and they'd both be brutally tortured until Le Roux grew bored with their screams and dumped their bodies out behind the latrines.

One good thing about her knowing would be the ability to send reports via the watch from his hut. Another would be the ability to control her. If she was aware of the situation, she was more likely to trust him and react well when things got chaotic. And, considering there was no plan on the table, it was going to get very, very chaotic.

The file was a disappointment. Some aerial shots a little more recent than the ones they'd had. Some intel that might help with a war-crimes trial, but nothing that would help them storm the beaches, so to speak. And no hint at the agent's identity, not that they'd be able to get that info to Donovan, anyway.

But Gallagher did find a few tidbits. Le Roux's trucks used a lot of gas and he'd had underground fuel tanks installed in the compound. Probably thought they were safer. The government's agent had helpfully marked their location, along with which hut housed the bulk of their ammunition.

He'd also detailed the extreme security around the rocket launchers Le Roux had set up after a badly botched aerial assault by the government. Nothing short of a small army could get to those.

"You guys need to get out there and do whatever it is documentary film crews do pretty soon," Carmen said. "We don't know where Le Roux has people and we don't want our arriving on Donovan's heels to raise suspicion."

Rossi nodded. "But we don't know how long we have before Donovan calls—*if* he's able to call—so we need something to throw at him."

Gallagher tapped one of the aerial shots. "I keep going back to this cliff. They've got a false sense of security about it, even though it's not high. See this? The perimeter's intact, but the posts are a lot more spaced out."

Rossi knelt next to the coffee table to get a better view. "Can he get through?"

"Not without diverting the attention of everybody in the camp. Even that wouldn't do him much good because it's a long fucking walk back."

"Look at the shots. Every post has a Jeep or a truck."

"We have to go on the assumption Donovan'll be unarmed." Gallagher pointed to different photos arranged in a rough layout of the compound, feeling the slight rush that came with a possible plan. "Massive diversion at the front. Fuel tanks, probably. Donovan and the girl go up the cliff. Two agents coming in dark from the rear take *this* truck, do the pick up and get the fuck out."

"How close can we land a helicopter?"

He pointed. "Here. Outside of the rocket launchers, close enough to deploy from and to pick up, central to both the front and back. And they'll expect the truck to head the other way— toward the main road and the border."

"I'd hoped for a silent extraction."

"We always hope for that, but we've got to extract this hostage from two hundred or so well-armed, well-trained, highly paranoid guerilla soldiers. Any chance of utilizing local contacts?"

Rossi shook his head. "Nobody's going to touch a suicide run up against Le Roux."

"Okay. You man the bird, I'll stage the diversion then meet up with O'Brien and Olivera to retrieve Donovan and the package."

He met Carmen's startled glance with a clenched jaw. Of course she was surprised. A willingness to send her into jungle combat wasn't his usual *modus operandi.*

But there was no way to pull it off without her, so he'd said the words fast, like ripping off a bandage. And he knew O'Brien would take the lead. He didn't work with the guy often, but he'd tapped him for the Group for a reason. He was solid, and a top guy to go through the door with.

"Grace is going to kill me," Rossi said, seemingly unaware of the undercurrents in the room.

"If we come out of this alive," Gallagher told him. "I'll play whipping boy for you. And she's not stupid. She knew when you boarded the plane you wouldn't be able to stay clean while we played in the mud."

"What kind of diversion are we talking about?" Carmen asked, sliding closer to him to get a better look at the photos.

He might have been able to come up with something if her hair wasn't tickling his arm. "I don't know yet. The bottom line is that we need to communicate to Donovan that when things suddenly get crazy, he has to get Isabelle up that cliff."

Rossi took a minute to fill Carmen in on Donovan's potential climbing freeze. "It could be a really big problem at a really bad time."

She pulled the shot of the cliff closer. "Will we be close enough to assist?"

"We'll have our hands full securing the truck," Gallagher said. "Without the vehicle, none of it matters."

Rossi grabbed a water and went back to his seat. "If we can communicate the plan to Donovan, we might be able to judge by his response if he can handle it."

"No, we need to communicate to him he has no choice. There's a good chance it'll come down to him handling it or both of them dying."

Donovan crouched in front of Isabelle. One, he could talk in a very low voice and she could hear him and two, he wanted her to look at him. "I need you to listen to me, Isabelle."

Her blue eyes gave away her wariness, but she leaned closer.

"I'm here to get you out." He'd decided to compromise by not telling her his name. For now. That would be the easiest mistake for her to make—especially since she hadn't known him long enough to entrench the alias in her mind. "You don't need to know much, but you need to stay close to me, and if something starts happening, you have to trust me completely and do *exactly* what I tell you, when I tell you."

"I thought…you aren't going to trade guns for me?"

"We—the people I work with and I—we can't give these monsters guns. The offer got me in the door, but we can't back it up."

She looked him directly in the eye then, her uncertainty not clouding her sharp intellect. "He said I can't go until he has his guns."

"Which is why my team is working on another way to get you out. It's a risk telling you this. You *have* to pretend you don't know, or he'll kill us both. But the plan might be a little…spontaneous, and you need to know I'm on your side."

He watched her process that information, knowing how hard it would be for her to believe in him. "Is my father paying you?"

He sighed. Not knowing how loyal she was to her father, he didn't want to set the Devlin Group—and therefore himself—up as the enemy. "Your father was arrested, Isabelle. The government asked us to rescue you in exchange for his testimony against other people. His assets are frozen, so our payment will be his giving information to our government."

"So why won't the government pay you?"

"They probably won't want to be tied financially to the Matunisian situation." Donovan shrugged. "We'll be paid for the original job, but there's a good possibility this little field trip will end up pro bono."

"I don't understand. Why would your team risk their lives for nothing?"

"You're not nothing," he snapped, and then he softened the words with a sheepish grin. "And, actually, my team came to keep *me* alive when they couldn't talk me out of coming."

"Why me? There are people all over the world who need saving right this minute. Why did you come for me?"

Shit. How had he gotten backed into this conversational corner? What was he supposed to tell her? That he'd looked into her face on the computer screen and...what? Decided by saving her, he'd save himself? That bringing her home alive would chase all the other ghosts away?

"For those others who need saving right now, there are people out there to save them. Nobody else was willing to come to Matunisia."

Isabelle gave him a small smile, and it hit him like a kick to the chest. God, even scared and frizzy-headed, she was beautiful. "So you're like Obi-Wan? My only hope?"

The pressure sat on his chest, keeping his lungs from fully inflating. "Something like that."

Chapter Ten

The last thing Carmen wanted was to be alone with Gallagher, but with the way her luck was running, she wasn't surprised when Rossi and O'Brien disappeared to schmooze some new local contacts willing to trade stockpiled explosives for American dollars.

Even worse was knowing Rossi originally intended to take Gallagher with him until he gave the boss some kind of signal. He'd taken O'Brien instead.

It was obvious, no doubt to *everybody*, that Gallagher wanted some alone time with her, maybe to clear up the tension they'd practically been choking on since leaving New Hampshire.

Dammit, she'd known sleeping with the man would affect her job and she should have kept her damn pants on. It was only one night, though—one night she couldn't resist.

She hadn't expected there to be repercussions so soon, but here they were, with Alex Rossi of all people all up in their business.

Screw that. It royally pissed her off he'd manipulated the situation to be alone with her. She was here to do a job and Gallagher could man up and deal with that or he could hang out and talk to himself.

But pissed or not, she was keenly aware of how close he

was and how her body even now yearned for his touch. She ached just thinking about him pushing back from the computer and taking her in his arms again, holding her. Making her body feel things she'd stupidly thought she could live without.

Biting back a vicious curse, Carmen downed some bottled water and did some warm up stretches. It was time to remind her traitorous body what was important—work. While she might throw in some pleasure once in a very great while, there were only two things she demanded from her body. Strength and agility, the most basic tools for doing her job.

Something punishing, she decided. Something that would make her muscles long for rest rather than another Gallagher-induced orgasm. Since a good, hard run wasn't going to happen, she did the next best thing.

After kicking off her sneakers, she rested her hands flat on the floor, kicked up into a handstand and turned until her sock-covered toes rested lightly against the wall.

"What are you doing?" Gallagher asked, and though she couldn't see him from that angle, which was good, she could hear the amusement in his voice.

"One of the advantages men have over women is superior upper body strength. I try to keep the advantage to a minimum."

She blocked him out then, as she started the grueling vertical push-ups. Breathing was vital, and the exercise intense enough her body was too busy to keep up with its yearning.

"How many of those are you going to do?" he asked after awhile, and he didn't sound amused anymore.

The plan was to sweat him out of her system, but she reluctantly had to admit she couldn't do it. The man was so deep under her skin it was going to take more than a little perspiration to get him out.

She turned, then lowered her feet to the ground and stood upright—did some upper body stretching so her shoulders wouldn't tense up. "Don't you have anything better to do than watch me work out?"

"Probably, but nothing I *want* to do more. And if you're just looking to sweat we could…" He let the sentence die off, but the raised eyebrow filled in the blanks.

"I am *not* having sex with you here. We're supposed to be working, in case you've forgotten."

"I can do both. I'm pretty talented that way."

He was pretty talented in a lot of ways, but no way in hell was she saying that out loud. "It's over, Gallagher. Give it a rest."

Over? Not by a long shot. She could push him away as hard as she wanted—which would be pretty hard based on those push-ups she'd been doing—but he could push harder.

"When this is over, maybe we could take a couple of down days together. Hit the beach." Maybe swing by San Diego and introduce her to his family. "Frolic in the sand and all that crap."

"I'm not frolicking with you again. In the sand or anywhere else."

"So we just forget what happened between us? That's it?" She was really starting to tick him off. Her pulling away, he'd expected. Turning into a bitch, he hadn't.

"Nothing else is going to happen between us because I'm not quitting the Group. It's more than my job—it's what I do."

"Jesus, Carmen, I asked you for a date. I *never* asked you to give up your job."

"But you won't let me *do* it."

"Didn't I just assign you to go out in the jungle and get shot at? What the fuck more do you want from me?"

"If there was another agent here, you'd have sat me out."

"If that agent was more qualified for the task, then yeah. Instead of making shit up, why don't you clue me in on your real problem?"

She was pissed enough he'd have already ducked if she had something in her hand to throw. "I'm not making anything up. When the Group went after Anetakis, you benched me and sent in Charlotte, who had *no* field experience and—"

"I benched you because she had a connection to him and I wasn't sure where your relationship with Ludka stood."

"That's bullshit! Nobody has *ever* doubted my loyalty to the Group. You threw my integrity under the bus so you wouldn't have to admit to Charlotte you were afraid I'd get hurt. And *then* you tried to cut me out of this job."

"Matunisia's not place for a—"

"Screw you, Gallagher. You've been trying to babysit me for a long time. Which is not sexy, by the way. Can you imagine what you'd be like if we had a *real* relationship?"

The emphasis on *real* stung, but he didn't wince.

"I won't live my life in bubble wrap, no matter how much you try to wrap me up. And I'm so tired of trying to dodge your overprotectiveness. I may not be G.I. Jane, but I'm not Lois Lane, either."

She paused, as if she expected him to say something, but what? Was he supposed to promise to stop worrying about her? To stop having nightmares about all the ways her jobs could go wrong? Not happening.

"I can't stop caring whether you live or die, Carm."

"Of course not, but you can stop letting your personal

feelings affect your professional judgment."

He'd have beat his head against the wall if it wouldn't attract attention. "You need to get over thinking there are neat, airtight little boxes to keep everything separate. Professional relationships in this box. Personal feelings in that box. It's not like that. Real life's messy and all mixed up."

"I don't do messy. And...I'm never having kids."

"Ever?"

"Ever. I love my job and I intend to do it as long as I can and then I'm going to travel."

"What the hell does that have to do with this?" He knew he was getting loud but this woman drove him batshit crazy. Then he narrowed his eyes. "You're using my concern for you in the field as an excuse to keep me at arm's length without telling me the real reason."

She stood there glaring at him, her jaw clenched while she inhaled slowly. "There's no future for us and if we try and fail, it'll affect the job. It's *already* affecting it. Rossi took O'Brien instead of you because of me."

He would have laughed if he couldn't see how hard it was for her to talk about this. "I'm not asking you to marry me tomorrow. I just want to see each other. See where it goes. It could actually work out, you know."

She snorted. "Yeah, right. You're the All-American boy next door."

"Only if it's a pretty freakin' interesting neighborhood."

"I mean it. You bleed red, white, and blue. When I look at you, I can practically hear "The Star-Spangled Banner" and smell the apple pie. You're picket fences and minivans and a baked ham every Sunday."

"You say that like it's a bad thing."

"It's not. It's just not *my* thing." He watched her school her features in an expression of cool disinterest. "Look, it happened. The crash, the woods—most people have sex after a near-death experience. Let it go."

She was lying. He knew it as surely as he knew her eyes were the exact brown of hot fudge topping. But he was freakin' tired of fighting her for a chance, and he'd be damned if he'd beg.

Maybe the time had come to put any feelings he had for Carmen to rest. When they got back to the States he was going to find a cheap bar, a cheaper date, and sweat her out of his system.

Sometimes, between one tick of the second hand and the next, a man realizes he's made a fatal error.

The realization could be painful—finding out you should have zigged instead of zagged in a gunfight. It could be explosive, a rush of adrenaline that carried you through it.

For Jack Donovan, that realization was silent, a slight tightening of the skin that might have shown on his face were Le Roux not greedily flipping through the book for more to add to the tentative list of weapons they'd drawn up.

Isabelle Arceneau was no longer afraid.

It was a subtle vibe. Something in the way she carried herself, maybe. Something that said she felt a little safer than she had the day before.

And safe was last thing a young woman being held hostage by a bloodthirsty terrorist and loaned out as a sex toy to an arms dealer should feel.

"I could get twice as many M-16s," Le Roux grumbled.

"And they jam twice as often," he said easily while scanning the room. "If I provide you with substandard equipment—even at your request—you'll be less inclined to do business with me in the future."

While Mr. Sensitivity over there probably wasn't tuned in to the emotional states of his captives, the other women might pick up on the difference in Isabelle. And women who spent every second of every day in fear just might try to curry favor by throwing a fellow captive under the bus.

He had to get her out of the compound. Soon. And, though Le Roux was enjoying showing off his operation and haggling, Donovan could only linger so long without raising suspicion.

If he had to, he'd leave and pretend to return with the weapons. It would buy some time to come up with a more solid plan. He was afraid walking away from Isabelle—leaving her behind, knowing she wouldn't believe he was coming back—would kill him, though.

More importantly, he was afraid it would kill *her*.

But he'd have to hurt her to save her. Before he could talk himself out of it, he beckoned to her. "Get me some coffee."

His stomach turning, he slid the papers on which he was making long lists of Le Roux's demands closer to the edge of the table and waited. It took her a few minutes, but she approached with the metal mug while—thankfully—Le Roux still had his head bent over the catalogue.

Praying nobody saw, he slid his foot out and nudged her ankle, not enough to trip her, but enough to make her stumble. Coffee splashed over the pages.

Jack exploded out of his chair, shoving her hard onto the floor. "You stupid, clumsy bitch!"

She scrambled away, her eyes on the floor and tiny sobs catching with each ragged breath. Le Roux watched with unabashed interest.

"Get your ass back over here," Jack hissed, grabbing the soaked papers in one hand. "Look what you did."

Isabelle didn't look up. "I...I'm sorry."

Her voice was just a whisper and, though it killed him to do it, he grasped her short hair as best he could in his hand and hauled her to her feet. She whimpered, trying to cower from him.

"You should punish her, my friend," Le Roux goaded, his grin making Jack sick.

"Oh, I'm going to punish her. We're going to my room and once she's done proving to me just how goddamn sorry she is, she's going to stay down there on her knees and recopy every one of these fucking papers."

While Le Roux roared his approval, Jack dragged Isabelle, sobbing and trying to keep up, out of the great room.

Alex Rossi was pissed. As if it wasn't bad enough his team was in freakin' Matunisia—that he'd sent one of his guys blind into a guerilla warlord's compound—now he had some soap opera shit going on with the guy whose game was pretty goddamn important to this job.

Whatever had happened between them while he and O'Brien were off making contact with a guy who wanted to sell very few explosives for very many American dollars, it wasn't good. Carmen was emitting so much tension, Rossi was surprised she didn't fry the electronics.

And Gallagher... He'd gone cold, and Rossi didn't like that at all. Gallagher had shut parts of himself down and the team needed him at one hundred percent every second they were in this country.

Maybe he should lock them in the bedroom. Order them to have sex and not come out until the personal shit was laid to rest and they could concentrate fully on the job.

Probably not. But he had to do something. Even O'Brien was getting antsy and awkward around them, and that guy was hard to shake up. Having Gallagher take O'Brien's head off his shoulders for not being able to read Donovan's mind and explain why he'd gone off on the girl probably didn't help. Which one to talk to, though?

It wouldn't do any good to talk to Gallagher. Rossi knew where he stood. He'd been hung up on the woman for a long time and, after their jaunt through the woods during which he and Grace suspected a little extra R&R had gone on, she seemed to be shutting him down.

That left Carmen, so instead of going himself, he sent Gallagher with O'Brien to go over the helo to make sure nobody'd messed with it and figure out how to stow all the weapons they'd need.

Carmen had taken O'Brien's seat in front of the computers. "The audio seems to be down. I can't really make it out."

"That happens. There are a couple of places in the compound where something interferes with the signal."

She nodded, and he sat in the closest chair, not having the slightest clue what to say. He'd call Grace, but one look at his watch changed his mind. Damn time difference.

"So, this thing between you and Gallagher—"

"Has not affected my work."

Rossi hadn't gotten to his position by backing away from a sharp tone. "Yet."

She swiveled her chair to face him. "I told him nothing's

going to happen here. If he can't handle that and it effects his job, that's his problem. And his lecture, not mine."

Since the stern schoolteacher routine wasn't going to get him squat, he changed tactics. "You know Grace and I were partners—and lovers—before."

"Of course."

"It wasn't always easy, but it's doable."

"But your relationship ended when...you know." Yeah, when he'd shot her and she'd disappeared, leaving him and the Group far behind her. "What if you'd ended your relationship and still tried to work together?"

Now he was getting somewhere. "I trust Gallagher to keep his professional and his personal crap separate."

"I guess if he was any good at that, you wouldn't be having this talk with me right now, would you? And if we did get together? He doesn't respect me enough to let me do my job without trying to protect me."

"One, if Gallagher didn't respect you, you wouldn't work for me. Period. Second, he's going to try to protect you whether he gets in your pants or not. We're men and, call me a sexist asshole, but we have this primitive urge to protect our women."

"Sexist asshole. But look how this is affecting things right now. Imagine if we're together for months or even years, and then we break it off. How much worse would it be?"

"I don't think you'd break it off. I think you guys would be good for each other." She wanted to believe that, he could see it in her face. "And if you did break up, you'd work separate assignments until you got over it."

"Yeah, but—"

"Yeah but nothing. We could sit here for an hour and you'll just keep coming up with bullshit excuses for not taking a chance on the guy."

Crimson burned up her neck into her cheeks, and Rossi wondered if she'd swing at him. Probably not, but he was ready to duck. "They're not bullshit. I don't want to have to choose between him and my job."

"I'm the boss, and I won't let you choose between him and your job. You're one of the Devlin Group's most valuable assets and I'm not letting you go. But where you guys are right now, it's not working. For anybody. Talk to him."

"I don't think there's anything left to say."

"You'll think of something. Talking's like breathing to women."

She laughed and, much to his relief, some of the tension was broken. "Sexist asshole."

Chapter Eleven

Jack closed the door to his quarters behind them and slid down to the floor, taking Isabelle with him. She didn't try to pull away, but she was curled up, trying not to touch him.

"I'm sorry," he whispered into her hair. "So, so sorry, honey."

Her tears splashed on his arms, and his throat tightened. He'd had to do it, he reminded himself. He was the one who'd fucked up and told her who he was. Now he'd bear the guilt.

He tried to stroke her hair and she flinched. He'd known that would break her down more than anything else—had known what the painstaking process of singing her hair off had meant to her—and that was why he'd done it.

"I had to do that, Isabelle. I didn't want to, but...you looked more confident. Too safe." She didn't move, so he kept talking. "I shouldn't have told you who I was. It was a risk, but I wasn't going to...I couldn't rape you and that's what I was expected to do.

"I thought you'd react better if things get crazy, too, if you trusted me. But you didn't look afraid anymore and if somebody wondered why and told Le Roux, he'd kill us both."

Her chest was no longer hitching with smothered sobs, but he could feel the fear in her body. "Honey, hurting you is the last thing I would ever want to do."

He shut up then, afraid he'd make it worse, and just held her. Slowly, very slowly, she relaxed against him. He stroked her hair lazily, trying to be as gentle as possible.

"You tripped me," she finally said. Her voice was still on the faint side, but the accusation felt good. She still had some fight in her.

"I know. But if I'd just explained what you were doing, I don't know if you'd have understood. I needed to...you've been conditioned and I needed to trigger that."

She tilted her head back to look up at him and it struck him again just how beautiful she was. "Deep down, under the...conditioning or whatever, I knew you wouldn't hurt me."

He stroked her cheek with the side of his thumb and her eyes slid closed, a small smile playing around the corners of her mouth. "It's been so long since I've been held by somebody who cares about me, Hans."

Jack. My name is Jack. He tightened his arm around her, pulling her closer to his chest. He did care. And every minute he spent with her, he cared more.

There was no room for caring in their situation.

"What now?" she whispered.

He had to clear his throat before he could answer her. "I'll buy you a little time away from the others by making you recopy those lists, then I'll try to come up with something else. I need you to be aware of your facial expressions and body language every single second we're not alone, though."

She nodded, then burrowed her head under his chin. It was killing him. Slowly.

He took a deep breath and tried to kill his burgeoning attraction for her. She was young. Traumatized. Of course she was clinging to him. He was the first person who'd been kind to her in almost two years.

"Can you stay here for a little while?" she asked in a small voice. "I feel safe with you. I haven't felt safe in a long, long time."

"I'm not leaving you," he said, and he'd never meant anything as much as he meant those words. No way in hell was he leaving this compound without her.

It was another two days of haggling before Le Roux finally asked the magic question—could he get weaponized anthrax?

Donovan hid his relief with a small shrug. If Le Roux hadn't asked, he would have had to find a way to bring it up himself. It was a lot less suspicious this way. "I have to call my supplier to check for availability."

The warlord narrowed his eyes and leaned back in his chair. "I thought you trusted nobody."

Jack shrugged. "I failed chemistry, so I have to go to a supplier for chemical weapons."

"Too bad, then, that the battery for your phone has been...depleted." Smart move, removing the power source for the only electronic device he'd brought—that his men found, anyway.

"I know the number. Hand me your phone."

After giving him the Evil Overlord stare, Le Roux set his phone in the middle of the table and activated the speakerphone. Jack reached over and punched in the number.

"Thank you for calling Astrid Pharmaceuticals. How may I direct your call?" Charlotte asked in a fast, chipper voice.

"Arnold Rogan."

"One moment please, sir, and I'll connect you."

About twenty long seconds of bad music, and then

O'Brien's voice. "Arnold Rogan speaking."

"Hello, Arnie."

"Hans? Oh, geez, man, I'm in the lab." Sure enough, in the background were the slightly tinny sound of voices and some scattered beeping.

"I need a delivery."

"I don't know, man. My courier's gone under. I got another guy—Chris Walker. It's been about seven years since I used him, but I trust him. Given him a lot of rope, and he ain't hung himself yet."

Acid bit into Jack's stomach, but he did his best not to show it. *Chris.* They wanted him to climb the freakin' cliff.

Not just climb the cliff, but get Isabelle up with him.

"I don't know about that," he said. Even if they had a rope in place for him, it was risky. What if he froze and the two of them were stuck on the wall like flies waiting to be swatted?

"Man, that's like the only courier I got."

Gallagher was the man behind the plan, but as soon as the cliff went into play, Rossi would have clued him in on the climbing situation. O'Brien using the name like that was proof they all knew what had gone down. If they needed him to do it anyway, that was the only hand they were holding.

"He better be solid. Do you have a timeframe for the delivery?"

"Jeez, man, lemme think. Umm...probably four days if I hustle. Make a nice diversion from reading biorhythms and watching the rats twitch, know what I mean?"

The diversion would come much sooner than four days. Sometime between three and five in the morning, when their biorhythms would be at their lowest point. "Usual arrangements. If the Walker fellow's fee is higher, that comes from your cut."

"I hear ya, man."

Jack reached out and disconnected the call. "Done."

Le Roux laughed and gestured for more drink. "Most excellent news, my friend! You will tell me how best to use it, no?"

"Of course. My reputation is based on satisfied clients. Blindly handing over a biological weapon and getting a client killed would be bad for business."

So would getting Isabelle killed if he choked halfway up the face of the cliff.

Gallagher penciled another dot on the grid in front of him, then sat up straight with a groan and rubbed his temples.

Coming up with a plan for one man to distract two hundred armed guerillas while one climbing-shy guy carried a damsel in distress up the side of a cliff wasn't his idea of fun.

But he had one. More or less.

Despite the extra helping of *oh shit* their local guys had served up. Technology had apparently skipped over the Matunisian black market and, while he had the explosives to make some pretty big booms, he'd have to trigger those booms by hand. Not a timed or remote detonator to be found.

Nothing he hadn't done before, but it meant one big, unhappy change in the plan—he wasn't going to be able to rendezvous with O'Brien and Carmen. The two of them had to take the truck and retrieve Donovan and the girl. Still doable, just a lot more gut-churning for all of them.

Then there was the fact Le Roux's people were night owls. Late to bed and late to rise meant to catch them at their most vulnerable, it would be an attack close to dawn. With an almost full moon. While it meant the team wouldn't have to mess with night vision equipment, it also meant the guerillas wouldn't need it, either.

"Rossi's up," Carmen told him, and he realized with a start she was sitting next to him. He was more tired than he'd thought. "Time to get some rest."

It'd be best to look over the grid with a fresh eye, anyway. He started to nod, but the strain of hunching over the coffee table for hours locked up the muscles in his neck and he winced.

Carmen was instantly on her feet. She took his hands and hauled him upright. "I'll rub you down as you go to sleep."

He couldn't handle her hands on him. Not after she'd shut him down so forcefully—after he'd decided to let it go. "I'm good."

"No, you're not. And you need to be." She shoved him into the bedroom and closed the door behind them. He flopped facedown on the bed, trying to will away the pain in his shoulders.

The mattress moved as she knelt next to him and he forced himself not to react when her hands started kneading between his shoulder blades.

"I...I've wanted to talk to you anyway," she said.

"No talking. You've said enough." He was exhausted and wasn't up to a relationship discussion. Or any discussion. "You've made it pretty clear you think I'm some kind of petty asshole who would destroy your career if you quit sleeping with me."

When she lifted her hands, he thought maybe he'd managed to drive her away. It was for the best.

But then her fingers were there again, easing the kinks out of his neck. "I don't think that."

She could have fooled him, but he kept his mouth shut. He was tired enough he might say something he couldn't take back. He might tell her how he *really* felt. If he did that, things would get a lot more awkward than they already were.

"My mom died when I was little. I went into foster care," she told him, a softness in her voice that told him, in a rare moment of male clarity, his best move was to keep quiet and let her talk. "I was lucky. I went to great homes. But the first couple, they moved out of state and I couldn't go. The next family, they really loved me, but their son died and...they couldn't deal. Another family gave me up when they adopted a sibling group.

"I learned a long time ago that everything ends. No matter how much somebody cares, nothing's really forever. And...you're the first person in so long—since I was a little girl—who has the power to hurt me.

"I know you're not a petty asshole, John. But if I let myself care about you—*really* care about you—when it ends, it'll hurt."

He rolled over so he could see her face. So she could his. "Everybody hurts when a relationship ends, babe. But it's worth the risk because sometimes it *doesn't* end. Sometimes it's forever and after the work is done and the world's been seen, there are two rocking chairs side by side on the front porch."

"The one on the house with the white picket fence?" She tried to smile, but it was more of a quiver.

"That's the one." He pulled her down next to him and got a little hopeful when she only offered a token resistance. "Stay with me."

She gave him a short, disbelieving laugh. "I don't think so."

"I'm not asking you to have sex during an op with our boss

120

on the other side of the door." He tugged on her until she lifted her head so he could wrap an arm around her. "Just let me hold you so I can get some sleep. I sleep better when you're beside me."

But she fell asleep first and he kissed her hair before nodding off himself.

Pain. Panic. Chris's hand twisting, grasping. He tried to hold him, dug his fingertips into Chris's wrist.

Slipping. He couldn't hold him.

Muscles stretching, tearing. If Chris could get his other arm up. Just...reach...up.

The weight gone. Oh god, Chris's face as he fell away.

Chris disappeared with one blink, replaced by beautiful, worry-filled blue eyes. "Hans, wake up. It's just a bad dream."

Hans? Who the hell was...

Jack took a shuddering breath and tried to focus on the present. "Did I shout anything? Was I loud?"

If he'd been loud enough to attract attention, they might have company they weren't ready for. They were both wearing too many clothes, for one thing.

"No," she whispered. "You were crying, but almost silently. Your whole body was shaking, though, and that's what woke me up."

"I'm sorry I disturbed you." He scrubbed his hand over his face, feeling the light sheen of sweat. "It's been a long time since I've dreamed about...since I've had that particular dream."

He didn't have the strength to pull away, or even give a token protest, when she scooted close to him and laid her head against his shoulder.

Just to comfort her. Maybe himself.

"Do you want to talk about it?" she asked.

Hell no, he didn't want to talk about it. *Hey, did I ever tell you how my best friend died because I wasn't strong enough to hold him?* Not exactly his style of pillow talk.

"Not really. It's just an old nightmare." But it shook him enough so he stupidly raised his arm so she could get closer and he could hold her.

Isabelle snuggled against his chest and Jack closed his eyes, savoring the feel of her against his body. He should send her back to her side of the bed. He should feign sleep and pray the real thing came eventually.

Instead, he turned his head and rested his face against the soft fuzz of her hair. She sighed and rested her hand on his chest, and he thought it was odd such a small gesture should kick his pulse into overtime.

Gritting his teeth and willing his body back into submission, Jack forced his focus back onto the mission. He was here to save her, nothing else. And to do that, he might just have to share his nightmare after all.

Isabelle needed to know she might be putting her trust in a man who didn't deserve it.

"Listen," he said into her hair, "there's a good chance to get out of here, we're going to have climb the cliff behind the compound."

"Like in that movie with Sylvester Stallone? Do you know how to do that?"

More like that movie than he'd care to admit under normal circumstances. "You know that scene in the movie where he's trying to hold that girl and he can't?"

"Yeah."

"Something similar happened to me three years ago, only he was my best friend. He...he screamed my name over and over until he hit." There was more he needed to tell her, but nothing else was getting past the lump in his throat right then.

"And that's what you were dreaming about?"

Jack nodded, then swallowed hard and cleared his throat. "I haven't been able to climb since, so you need to know I...I might freeze up on you or freak out. If that happens, you need to get yourself up that cliff. My people will be at the top and they'll take care of you."

She wasn't much for fidgeting as a rule, but he felt her grow even more still against him. "I've never gone climbing before. Not even an indoor rock wall."

"Your instincts will guide you if you let them. Don't overthink it or second-guess your gut." Her body was relaxing against his again, and he knew it was only a matter of minutes before she slid back into sleep.

"I know you'll save me," she mumbled. "Just like I know if it was at all humanly possible to save your friend, you would have. I don't think you have it in you to let somebody down."

"Don't go slapping some kind of hero sticker on me, Isabelle," he warned. "I'm not Superman."

"No," she said softly against his chest, "you're my Obi-Wan."

As they lay there in the dark hut and her breathing slowly grew deeper and steadier, he didn't have the heart to remind her Obi-Wan died in the first act.

Chapter Twelve

Gallagher sighed and leaned back in his chair. "She sounded pretty damn close to the audio mic."

"She did," O'Brien agreed. They kept their voices low because Carmen was in the other room sleeping and Rossi had finally crashed on the couch. "How far gone do you think he is?"

"Far enough to second-guess his judgment when it comes to her."

"But we should trust yours when it comes to Olivera?"

Gallagher didn't take offense. Hell, back in New York he'd practically said straight out he didn't trust his own judgment when it came to her being in the field.

"She'll be with you," he told O'Brien, "so it's your judgment that matters."

"You know I'll do my best to bring her back in one piece."

He did *not* want to have this conversation. O'Brien talking about bringing Carmen back in one piece was too vivid a reminder the possibility existed she might *not*. "Make the best call for the situation. She'll bring herself back."

O'Brien nodded. "You figure out where you're putting the charges?"

"Yeah." They were like timed firecrackers, designed to simulate the gunfire of a smallish army. "And I'll blow the front tanks first. Once Donovan's up the cliff I'll blow the reserve tanks in the rear—drive them away from the area."

He could picture the entire operation in his mind and it would work. Assuming everybody did everything they were supposed to do when they were supposed to it, which very rarely happened in real life.

"Rossi on comm?" O'Brien asked.

"Yeah, but Charlotte will be running the show from Texas. No way in hell I'd try something like this without her."

She was going to earn her money, for damn sure. To keep the chaos under control, all audio would be fed to Charlotte, who would then pass necessary info between the agents. Multiple agents in multiple locations in possible multiple gunfights all shouting over one another never helped.

O'Brien chugged some water and scrubbed his eyes. "No chance at all of incapacitating the rocket launchers?"

"No. He was smart enough to protect the hell out of those outposts. At this point, it is what it is."

Gallagher closed his eyes, picturing every agent. Every step. Between the planning and the coming prep work, he'd done everything he could. God willing, it was enough.

Carmen went about the business of looking like a documentary maker breaking down camera equipment, but the awareness of what Gallagher was about to do grew stronger with every second, until she could barely hear over the roaring in her ears.

When they packed up and drove back to the hotel, they'd be going without him. He'd be spending every second of darkness reconnoitering and prepping the area for Donovan's extraction. The same area occupied by Le Roux and his men.

And the bastard was laughing. He and O'Brien were actually cracking jokes as they checked Gallagher's gear. Yes, she knew that's how they readied themselves, but this time the lightheartedness grated on her nerves.

Once she and O'Brien drove away, she wouldn't see Gallagher again until it was over. Assuming everything went according to the half-ass plan they'd concocted—the one that could go wrong in a hundred different and fatal ways.

Carmen tried to concentrate on breaking down and stowing the camera equipment that was part of their cover, but she couldn't shake the really bad feeling that was churning her stomach and making her hands tremble badly enough so she fumbled a battery pack.

She was coiling the last of the cords when, through her peripheral vision, she saw O'Brien shake Gallagher's hand, then slap him on the shoulder.

Oh God. They were done. It was time to leave him behind.

As Gallagher approached her, pride made her suck it up and after a few seconds she was calm enough to meet him halfway.

"Time for you guys to hit the road," he said. "Remember what I said—stay close to O'Brien. Be aware of where he is and put a bullet in anything else that moves."

She nodded, not sure she could actually speak. There was nothing soft about him at that moment. The man who could charm the knickers off a nun was gone, leaving behind the warrior who was totally focused on his mission.

As he should be. Now wasn't the time to distract him with her own fears and...whatever it was she was feeling. If she couldn't even sort it out herself, there was no sense in dragging him into it.

"So...that's it, I guess," he said and, after a moment of

126

looking uncertain as to whether or not he should shake her hand or slap her ass or what, he shrugged. "See ya on the flipside, babe."

"Don't call me babe," she said automatically, and he winked at her over his shoulder as he walked away. Panic squeezed her chest. She wasn't done yet. "John!"

He stopped, but didn't turn. His shoulders hunched just for a second, as though he'd taken a blow, and then they straightened and he looked back at her.

"I can't do this right now, Carm. You're killing me and there's no room for it here. Not today." He started away again, shaking it off.

She knew that, but she couldn't have stopped herself. She couldn't let him go without some acknowledgement of what was between them. Not that she knew what it was or what she even wanted it to be, but there was *something*.

He stopped again. "God-*damn*-it."

He turned back and in four long strides she was in his arms. He lifted her, yanking her body against his as his mouth claimed hers. Carmen breathed him in, feeling his strength and determination washing over her.

She clung to him, even when the kiss ended, burying her face in his neck. He stroked her hair, then tipped her chin up so she could see his face.

"When this is over, will you let me take you to dinner?"

Her heart skipped. "Like a date?"

"Yeah, some of that normal-type stuff guys do you were talking about."

"I'd like that."

He smiled, that carefree, naughty smile that knocked her socks off. "Then I'll definitely be back."

"I believe you." When he looked at her like that, all fierce and ready to go off to war, she did.

"You can always believe in me, babe." Then he turned and walked into the woods where they'd stowed his gear.

"Don't call me babe," she called after him and his laughter lingered behind him.

While Rossi flew the chopper as fast and low as he dared in the dark, Carmen strapped her vest and matching knee-length chaps over her jumpsuit.

They weren't exactly fashionable, but they were state-of the art, lightweight and bulletproof. Designed to protect her vital organs and femoral arteries, they were still flexible enough not to constrict her movement. Everybody on the team was wearing them, even Rossi, who'd be staying with the helicopter.

"Gallagher checked in." Charlotte's voice was low in their earpieces. "It's a go."

Good news, but she'd rather hear it from Gallagher himself. Knowing he was out there, sneaking around in Le Roux's jungle had cost her some of her battle nap, despite his checking in whenever he could.

"You okay, Carm?"

She looked over at O'Brien, who was going through the same gearing up she was. "I'm good."

"Anything you wanna go over?"

She smiled. "Anything *you* wanna go over?"

He laughed and shook his head. "Just let me lead, try to stay in my sightline and keep me in yours."

Nodding, she stowed her .22 in her thigh pocket. She'd carry a Heckler & Koch G36 tonight, but the only thing she did without her little Ruger close at hand was shower. Like a cold and lethal security blanket.

"Carmen." He said nothing else until she made eye contact. "You have nothing to prove to me or anybody else on this team. Don't try to be Wonder Woman, just follow my lead and watch your ass."

Or Gallagher'll have mine. He didn't need to finish that thought. No doubt he'd been given an earful on how to properly secure the bubble wrap.

She gave him a quick nod to let him know she heard him, but her mind was already back on Gallagher—right back where it shouldn't be at a time like that.

What if she was the one with the authority? Would she have wavered on sending him alone into hostile territory at night? Sent O'Brien instead?

Turning her attention to tightening the laces of her boots so O'Brien couldn't see her face, Carmen forced herself to consider the question.

If she had the power, would she use it to keep Gallagher out of harm's way?

It had nothing to do with respect, she realized now. God knows she respected the hell out of Gallagher's ability to do his job.

Something to think about—

"Showtime," Rossi said.

Later.

As signals went, four five-hundred gallon tanks of gasoline exploding at two-thirty in the morning were pretty hard to miss.

Donovan's feet hit the floor as Isabelle sat upright on the bed, groggy and confused.

"Put your shoes on," he hissed. They'd been sleeping fully dressed. Besides encouraging him to keep his hands to himself, they were also ready to move in seconds.

"It's time, isn't it?" She was shaking, trying to focus, and he put his hands on her shoulders to steady her.

"Another minute or so to let them get focused on the front of the camp, and then we're going."

"I'm scared, Hans."

"Jack," he said, tightening his grip just a bit. "My name is Jack Donovan."

She stepped forward, closing the distance between them. He stiffened, then wrapped his arms around her and held her for as long as he dared. Tears glistened on her eyelashes when he pulled back.

"I'm ready," she whispered. "If we live through this, promise me I'll see you again."

"We'll live," he said, avoiding making a vow he didn't think he should keep. There were so many reasons to stay away from her he couldn't articulate just one. "You do exactly what I tell you, and we'll live."

Sadness flickered in her eyes—she'd noticed the omission and didn't understand her feelings for him weren't real. "If I stay I'm going to die anyway, so I might as well go for it, right?"

He was quiet for a few seconds, listening as the chaos moved beyond their hut and toward the front. In the distance he could make out the rapid burst of machine gun fire and he wondered how Gallagher had made it sound like there was an entire army bearing down on the encampment.

"When I say go, you follow me out the door, and stay behind me. It's going to be dark in places. Keep your hand on my back and if you trip and fall, don't scream."

"I'm sorry you have to go through this for me."

He smiled. "I'm not. Now...*go.*"

Gallagher moved through dense leaves, listening as Charlotte quietly and calmly relayed information between Rossi and the other agents.

He knew Carmen and O'Brien were approaching the outpost on the cliff by foot, on schedule. He knew how many seconds until the next charge went off—charges designed to keep Le Roux's guerillas occupied toward the front of the compound, away from the cliff and in the opposite direction of the helicopter.

The increased activity and heightened panic fractured the guerillas' attention, allowing him to slip unnoticed through the jungle.

"Gallagher," Charlotte said, "you need to be en route to extraction point now."

"On my way." Reluctantly, and dragging his feet the entire way.

What he wanted to do was work his way over to Carmen, roll her up in industrial bubble wrap and get her the hell out of Matunisia. But if he didn't stick to the plan, he wouldn't reach the rendezvous point ahead of the truck and they'd have to risk being Swiss-cheesed or leave without him.

Neither appealed, so he veered off toward his escape route, forced to trust Carmen to do her job and O'Brien to keep her safe. If everything went according to plan, they'd be leaving Matunisia within the hour.

Screaming. Gunfire. Shouting. More explosions. It was like navigating hell without a GPS.

Jack ran, keeping close to the buildings, with Isabelle's hand pressed against his lower back. He could feel her there, knew she was keeping up.

As he ran he scanned the cliff, sporadically lit by the fires, trying to think like Gallagher. If he'd been able to drop a rope, where would it be?

There. Angled away from the camp, deep vertical crevices and vegetation offering shadows.

He took a sudden left, Isabelle's hand never leaving his back. The camp around them was in chaos, nobody seeming to find it odd that two people were running in the dark.

When they reached the edge of the camp, however, he slowed them, taking a few seconds to look around. He could hear the gunfire at the top of the cliff, knew at least a couple of Devlin Group agents were up there, waiting for them.

"See that dark ridge running up the cliff over there?" He pointed and she nodded. "If they were able to drop a rope, that's where it'll be. If not, there are cracks and trees. On my go, run and don't stop until you get to the top."

She nodded again, fear shimmering in her eyes. "You'll be right behind me, won't you?"

Maybe. "Absolutely. Now... Go!"

In the short distance to the base of the cliff, no shots or shouts rang out in their direction. Less than a minute later, he found the rope and breathed a sigh of relief when he saw all the knots tied into it. They'd make it easier—hell, they'd make it *possible*—for Isabelle to make the climb alone if she had to.

"Use the knots, hand over hand. It'll be faster to walk up the wall, but if you get tired or slip, lock onto a knot with your feet, just like in gym class."

She didn't hesitate and, once again, Jack admired her

courage. They had no idea what was waiting for them at the top, but this was their only chance and she didn't waste any time crying or wringing her hands.

They were halfway up when a shot ricocheted off the rocks, startling Isabelle. Her concentration broke and she slipped, but caught a knot between her feet, just as he'd instructed.

In his mind she kept slipping. Falling. Her fingernails would gouge his wrists as she tried to hold on.

He wouldn't be able to hold her. Which name would she scream as she fell?

Jack? Or Hans?

"Jack! Keep climbing! Jack! You're here with me. Stay with me."

He wanted to tell her he knew where the hell he was, thank you very much, but his freakin' jaw wouldn't unclench.

"One hand over the other, Jack."

For chrissake, he knew how it was done. He'd been climbing since before she was born. *Jesus*, maybe literally. No. He did the math. It was close, but no.

"Please, Jack. *Oh God.*"

Couldn't she see he was trying? No, probably not. Just the sweat and the trembling, and she'd probably notice when he tossed his dinner in about two seconds.

"Your friends are waiting for us at the top." He could hear the panic edging into her voice and there wasn't a damn thing he could do about it. "They're here to help us, Jack, but we have to climb to get to them."

"Go," he managed, in such a low, teeth-clenched way she probably didn't hear him.

"No. Not without you."

Then she was going to die, and it would be his fault. Just

like Chris. Just like Carmen and O'Brien when they figured out he was a useless fuck-up and tried to come rescue Isabelle themselves.

No. Fuck no.

He shifted his weight, tested his grip. Swallowed back the searing acid of fear until he was fairly sure he could talk. "I'm...okay. Let's go."

She only went a few feet before looking down to see if he was lying.

"Don't stop," he barked. If he stopped he might not be able to start again.

The next, inevitable bullet hit two feet to the left of Isabelle's head and she screamed. Slipped again, hit him hard. He tightened his grip, holding both their weight.

The panic clawed at his brain, but the adrenaline kicked onto high gear. This was now, and right now he wasn't going to let Isabelle die. "You're okay. *We're* okay. Take a breath and then climb."

"I can't. Ohmigod, they're shooting at us."

"It's a lot harder to hit a moving target, and we can't go down. If you want to live, you have to go up. *Move.*"

Carmen moved, fired, moved again, struggling to keep her focus in the chaos.

"Four o'clock!" O'Brien shouted.

She spun, found her target and fired. There were only half a dozen guys at this guard post, and her partner was doing a fine job of dispatching them, but Donovan needed to get that girl up the cliff before their friends from neighboring outposts came to see what was going on.

A bullet whizzed by, a little too close, and she threw herself sideways. She whacked her elbow on a rock, but rolled and fired. Another movement and she spared the half-second necessary to register it wasn't O'Brien, then shot that guy, too.

"They're climbing," Charlotte reported through their earpieces.

Thank God for Donovan's watch, Carmen thought. At least they knew they weren't doing this for nothing.

Then a glimpse of movement far off in the trees to the east caught her eye. *Shit.*

"More company coming," she said to O'Brien. "I'll hold them off while you help haul them over the edge."

O'Brien was a better shot, but he was physically stronger and there was no telling what shape the girl was in.

She moved away from the cliff edge—away from the truck—and took up a position that put a large rock in front of her and a cluster of trees behind her, then waited.

"They're almost to the top," O'Brien reported.

A half-dozen men were moving through the thin vegetation in front of her and Carmen took aim at the first. Fired. He dropped, but the others dove for cover.

"I have the package," O'Brien said and Carmen let out a short sigh of relief. It was almost over.

Then the guerillas opened fire on her.

Rossi listened, helpless and alone in the helicopter, as the plan went totally, irrevocably, to shit.

Charlotte: Opening all comms now.

Olivera: I'm under fire.

O'Brien: Package is on board. Move it, Carmen.

Gallagher: Get your ass on that truck!

Olivera: I'm pinned!

O'Brien: Jesus! Jack, get her down on the floor. Trucks coming in from the north. We're under heavy fire.

Gallagher: Throw the girl on the floor and get a gun, Donovan!

O'Brien: We can draw them away, but we'll be boxed in if we don't go *now.*

Donovan: Move, O'Brien!

Olivera: Go! I'll find a way to get out.

Gallagher: No!

Donovan: Jesus Christ, O'Brien! Get us the fuck out of here!

Olivera: Get the girl out of here.

Gallagher: O'Brien, you motherfucker, you wait for her!

O'Brien: Status?

Olivera: Pinned. Go now!

Gallagher: *Shit!*

O'Brien: Package is en route.

Gallagher: You hold on, Carmen. I'm coming.

Chapter Thirteen

Plan A—balls to the wall through the compound, guns blazing as he mowed down any Matunisian motherfucker who got in his way.

Go...go...go... The urge pounded through Gallagher's brain, demanding he haul ass, but he resisted. Stayed hidden. If he got killed, she would die. That plain, that simple.

Focus, goddammit. He breathed in through his nose and exhaled through his mouth, driving back the adrenaline-fueled rage by force of will.

Plan B. A methodical, stealthy, ammo-conserving move in her direction. Not slow, but careful. A few more precious seconds to center himself—to immerse himself once more in his surroundings—and he began to move. A wider path than he would have liked, but most of Le Roux's men were focused around the compound.

"My gun jammed," Carmen said in his earpiece. Thankfully she kept her voice low so the guerillas didn't know, but he could hear the tinge of panic. "I can't...*shit*, I can't clear it."

"All right. Can you lift a weapon from a DB? Any near you?"

"No. I can't move." He heard the deep breath, and her voice was calmer when she spoke again. "I have my .22, so I'm not unarmed."

As good as, with nothing but that. Hell, she might as well chuck fucking rocks at them. "Is it light enough to they can get a good look at you?"

"I can see them, so they can see me. There's not much canopy here, so it's getting light fast."

"Here's what I want you to do," he responded with an absolute confidence that was absolute bullshit. "You have your hair braided?"

"Yeah, I always do. What the hell does—"

"Lose the braid, put your hair in one of those ponytail things. Take the vest off, drop the top of your jumpsuit and tie the arms around your waist, like you would if you were hot."

"And how is hangin' out in my sports bra going to...oh. No. No. No."

"They won't kill you if they want to—" He couldn't say it. "Just do it, Carmen. Let them get a glimpse of you."

"And if they get their hands on me?"

"Every second you're not dead is another second I have to get there, babe." A bullet buzzed by his ear and he dropped. *Shit.*

He tuned out her mutterings about *a freakin' striptease in the middle of the goddamn jungle* and scanned his surroundings. Nothing moved, a sure sign they were looking for him as hard as he was looking for them.

"Gallagher? Are you listening?"

A rustle in the underbrush. A loud ragged breath from some moron who'd held his breath trying to be quiet.

"Gallagher?"

The soldier saw him, but it was too late. Gallagher fired, then waited, listening.

Carmen froze in the act of trying to get out of her vest without sticking any body parts out in the open. "John?"

Being the newest sex toy on the guerilla block was bad enough on a temporary basis, but if Gallagher was... If he couldn't come for her...

If he couldn't come, she'd have to find another way to get herself out. As quickly as she could without breaking her cover, she tied the arms of her jumpsuit around her waist. Top half bare but for her black sports bra and the prickle of sweat, she strained to hear anything at all through her earpiece. A grunt. A breath, no matter how shallow.

Gunshots.

Carmen pulled off the rubber band and slid her fingers through her hair to unravel the tight braid. Then she gathered it high on her head and yanked it through the elastic.

"Okay, babe, I'm on the move again."

Her breath whooshed out of her and she picked up the .22. "Good, 'cause I'm about to flash the bad guys some Sitting Duck Barbie."

Before her brain could veto the insanity, Carmen popped out from behind the rocks, leading with the gun.

A spatter of return fire, then a couple shouts of surprise. Mission accomplished, she ducked back under cover, listening to the excited chatter of French.

Yes, *mon dieu*, she was a woman. Yeah, she had great tits, and that last guy? He was doomed to disappointment. But the debate on who was going to stick what where was keeping them busy.

"What's going on there, Carm?"

"Rock Paper Scissors for who does me first."

"Keeps their fingers off the triggers."

She dared a peek around the rock. "They're pulling back."

"Did they see your .22?"

"Yeah, when I shot it at them."

"They're going to move out of your range. Take potshots at you, make you burn through your ammo."

A tiny wisp of hope curled through her belly. "So I fire enough shots to make them think their plan is working, but not so many I run out of bullets before you get here."

"Even with the range, you can't slip away?"

"Not without them seeing me, but I'll have a head start if I need to run."

"Not yet. Nowhere to run to. But it won't be long before those guys have company."

"Maybe they won't want to share and I can slip away during their Civil War."

"I need you to—*shit!*"

Static. His comm was dead.

Jack shoved Isabelle's head down and held it there while O'Brien hit every rut and bump between the cliff and the helicopter.

The pinging of bullets against the truck from the pursuing guerillas grew less frequent, but O'Brien never let off the gas, careening along the narrow, moonlit jungle path as if he'd driven it his entire life. Since the truck was nothing more than an ancient, stripped-down, open-air safari Jeep, it wasn't a smooth ride.

"Ohmigod," Isabelle whimpered when the rear quarter panel slapped a tree in a particularly tight corner.

Jack stroked her hair, but his attention was on their

backtrail. "We got dirt bikes coming. Three, I think."

O'Brien swore into the mic. "We need to lose them before we meet up with Rossi in...maybe three minutes?"

"Stop when you find a good spot."

Isabelle lifted her head, her blue eyes wide with fear. "We're stopping?"

"If we don't stop them now, they'll stop us at the helicopter." He didn't elaborate, being a little busy taking stock of the weapons left behind by the truck's previous owners. A bunch of highly used shit, mostly.

"I'll take that one," Isabelle said, reaching around him for an old thirty-ought-six, of all things. "And those shells over there. They go with it."

"What the hell are you doing?"

"Hello...rich outdoorsman dad? Hunting expeditions, all that. I'm a good shot, and I can help."

Yeah, by curling herself into a tiny ball on the floor of the truck so he could concentrate. By being the smallest target she could be. "There's a big difference between shooting an animal and shooting a man, and I don't want you dealing with that on top of everything else."

She paused in the checking of her rounds like a pro. "There might be a difference between shooting an animal and a man, but trust me, there's not much difference between *these* men and animals."

"Stopping!" O'Brien shouted as the truck skidded to a stop.

Jack raised his weapon, trained on the breaks in the trees, hoping to take down their pursuers before they even knew they'd stopped.

A glimpse of chrome and Isabelle fired first. A shout and a bike tumbling. Jack caught the next guy and the one after that.

They spared a full thirty seconds, but didn't hear anymore coming.

He told O'Brien to go, then looked at Isabelle. Calmly, she flipped the safety on and reloaded the gun with hands trembling so slightly he almost didn't notice.

"Isabelle?"

She looked up at him and it was there in her eyes again— that calm and resolute strength he'd seen in the video of her, when she'd faced death with the determination at least she'd die well. "I'm okay."

There was no time to make sure of it as they broke into a clearing and the helicopter was there, fired up and ready to fly. O'Brien slid the truck to a halt and Jack jumped out of the back to catch Isabelle as she went after him.

He got her in her seat, strapped her in tight, aware that Rossi was exiting the cockpit.

"I'm staying," the boss said. "Get out of here."

A metallic thunk in the side of the helo and Jack heard Isabelle bite off a scream. Through the open door he saw them coming from a different direction—a couple of jeeps who'd probably wanted to cut off the escaping truck and instead had found a bigger prize.

"No time! Whole shitload of them on our ass," O'Brien shouted. "Take us up!"

"I can't leave them!"

"Don't be stupid." O'Brien shoved him toward the pilot seat. "They're alive. You get off this bird, you're not. You can't help them from here, but there won't be shit for help later if we're all fucking dead in this tin can."

For a few crazy seconds, Jack watched Rossi believe it was worth the risk, then he shouted something in Italian and went back to his seat. Another bullet struck near the door and Jack curled himself around Isabelle as the rotors picked up speed.

Finally they were in the air, leaving hell behind, and Jack kissed the top of her head. "You're safe now, honey."

Her body shook in his, and he tightened his arms around her. With danger dropping away behind them, he could breathe again. He'd done it.

"Charlotte," Rossi barked into his mic, "you find out who has what satellites up there and get me fucking eyes on that jungle. Anybody, I don't give a shit *who* it is, tells you no on this, I'll throw all the Group's resources into ruining him. You spread that around. Whatever you have to do to help us get them the fuck out of there."

As the smoke from the fires grew pale and small on the horizon, Jack sent a silent prayer out to whoever or whatever might be listening. He'd gotten Isabelle out.

But at what cost?

Five minutes passed with nothing but static, and Carmen started thinking a Plan B was in order. Or C or D or Q or whatever plan they were down to at this point.

Whether it was another false alarm or not, losing comm with Gallagher again drove home the fact he might not come and sitting around waiting to run out of ammo wasn't a great strategy.

She'd leave her hair in the ponytail, but she slipped her arms back into the jumpsuit and zipped it. Closing her eyes, she visualized the photo layout of the area they'd assembled. Where she was. Where the helicopter had been. Where Gallagher was supposed to have been and which way he'd be coming for her.

She was going to go a little wider out. As much as she wanted to run into him, she couldn't take for granted he'd be there to run to. One way or another, she needed to be closer to anywhere but here.

Scoping out the area behind her, Carmen noted the rocks, the trees. A deadfall. Groupings of leaf-heavy branches. No, this wasn't her element, but she could control one factor and that was herself. Silent and invisible. That was her job and she was damn good at it.

They'd fallen into a routine—the bad guys would take potshots at her, she'd fire back, then they'd laugh and stand around, smoking and continuing their argument on who was doing what to her first.

Just in case it was only his outgoing feed that was down, Carmen talked quietly into her mic, telling him what she was up to and where she hoped to be going. It helped calm her, helped her believe he was on the other end, listening. Probably cursing her. But there—still alive—just unable to communicate.

It would also tell Charlotte and the rest of the team where she was, not that there was a damn thing they could do about it.

Digging into one of the jumpsuit's many pockets, she pulled out a length of fishing line, then drew her knife. It took her a minute, but she managed to secure and saw off the bottom four inches of her ponytail. After finding a long enough stick within arm's reach, she tied the four inches of hair to one end of the stick and sharpened the other.

A bullet pinged off her rock, followed immediately by another, which buried itself in a tree trunk over her head.

She took a deep breath and readied herself. At this point she didn't have much to lose. She waited—there would be at least a half-dozen shots fired in her general direction—and then she stood.

Again she fired three shots, which didn't have a chance in hell of hitting them, and then they laughed. Again. She ducked down and tucked the gun away. If all went according to plan, she wouldn't need it. If things didn't go according to plan, it wouldn't be much help anyway.

She stuck the stick into the ground, making sure the end of the gathered hair was just visible over the top of the rock. People generally saw what they expected to see, and she'd help them along. The longer they thought she was crouched back there, the further away she'd be when they realized she wasn't.

It was hard work and took up the better part of three or four minutes, but Carmen managed to squeeze her body through the stand of trees behind her. With any luck, her friends wouldn't get bored enough to take shots at her for another five to six minutes. Then, when she didn't shoot back, they'd probably assume she was out of ammo, but they'd approach cautiously, just in case. That could buy her another five to ten minutes, which was more than enough.

Time to disappear and then—please, God, let her run into Gallagher.

Rossi put the helicopter down and Jack quickly dressed Isabelle in the traditional Matunisian women's wear Carmen had stowed under the seats, taking special care to hide her face.

They were monitoring Carmen, knew she was on the move, but they couldn't raise Gallagher and the tension was nearing the breaking point.

Rossi started for the door, but O'Brien stopped him with a hand to the chest. "We need to take a minute."

"I don't have a minute."

"We need to get the camera equipment and walk off this helicopter like we just got some great documentary footage and we're drafting our Oscar speech."

"Bullshit, let's—"

"We need this cover until they're out of the jungle and we can blow this popcorn stand."

Jack agreed, but he kept his mouth shut. The boss was running on emotion and adrenaline and if Jack got in his face, he was going to bear the brunt of it. Fair accusation or not, it was his and Isabelle's fault Rossi had left people behind. Rather than risk a blow-out, he'd let O'Brien do the talking.

Rossi sucked in a breath and scrubbed his face with his hands. "Okay. Just...get the shit and let's do this."

The walk to the Hotel Jardin was uneventful, much to Jack's surprise. It was a Murphy kind of day, and he took every step expecting the boogeyman to jump out of the shadows and grab them by the throats.

When they reached their room, he grabbed a bottle of water and a protein bar and hustled Isabelle straight to the bedroom. The curtains were already drawn, and he set the snack on the dresser.

"Stay in here, out of the way, and stay away from the window."

She nodded, her expression telling him she understood the situation was still critical. "Can I...can I take a shower?"

"Not yet. Take a nap if you want, but stay fully clothed." And, oh God, it was not the time for his mind to go *there*. "You need to be ready to move."

She was quiet until he turned to go and then her composure cracked. "Jack, I'm...please stay with me."

"I can't. I need to get back to my team. Gallagher and

Carmen are still out there and..." And it was his fault. "I'm going to have to go out, and I probably won't get a chance to say goodbye. Rossi will be with you. The Italian guy? You can trust him."

"You'll come back, right?" Her eyes were huge against her pale skin. "After your job is done, you'll come back here?"

He should tell her no. Tell her his mission was accomplished, Rossi would see about getting her a flight out and wish her a good life. "I'll try."

"Try hard, because I'll be waiting."

Chapter Fourteen

If somebody sneezed, Rossi was going to shatter into a million pieces. He knew it—knew he was wound too tight—but he couldn't take that internal step back.

"Talk to me, Charlotte," he told his exec admin over a closed comm channel while Donovan monitored Carmen. O'Brien was refueling the helo, making sure it was good to go with a second's notice.

"We owe favors to three countries, but I've got eyes. Every techie we have is monitoring some inch of jungle, but we haven't seen them yet. Tony wrapped up his job and he's watching the camp itself. They've almost got the fires contained and it looks like they're organizing to head out."

"But they haven't brought anybody in? Dead or alive, Le Roux would bring him in to—" He swallowed. Hard. "Goddammit."

"No, Alex. There's no sign of him. And if we even *think* we've got something, I'll let you know."

"I need a miracle here," he said, talking low so the nerves maybe wouldn't show. "I think he's used his up—the helicopter crash, finding that cabin, getting Isabelle Arceneau out of there... I think he's used up his allotment and we need to make a miracle *for* him. Somehow."

"We'll get...hold on. Hold on just a second, Alex."

He couldn't hold on. He needed to move, to *do* something, not be put on hold.

"We just caught a quick glimpse of Carmen through the treetops. She's moving away from the compound and she'll be out of range of the rocket launchers in...less than a mile."

"Hold on. Donovan, you go with O'Brien. Get that bird in the air and we'll figure out how to get her on it before you get there. Hopefully." When Donovan looked over his shoulder at the closed bedroom door, Rossi shoved him away. "I've got her. Get your ass in the air *now*."

It killed him to stay behind, but somebody had to stay with Isabelle Arceneau. And somebody had to be Plan C. If something happened to O'Brien and Donovan, it would be up to him to get Carmen out.

He owed Gallagher that much.

What the fuck was a Blue Jay doing in the middle of the Matunisian jungle?

Gallagher—working in the dark since his piece of crap, supposed-to-be-waterproof comm battery pack had shit the bed when he went down in a swampy area to avoid a bullet—stayed hidden. Somebody was watching him, he knew that much. But he didn't know who.

And there it was again. A freakin' blue jay.

Carmen. He had no idea if she could whistle bird calls, but it was a little farfetched for anybody else in the jungle to be mimicking arguably the most distinctive bird song in North America. Other than the loon, maybe, but loon calls were a bitch to imitate.

Taking a chance, he whistled a sound bite from a television show he knew they both watched. The show's counter-terrorism unit's phones had a distinctive ring and they'd both had it as their cell ringtones for a while.

When she whistled it back to him, he almost cried like a girl. She was alive and she'd managed to slip her leash. It damn near killed him, but he somehow kept his focus as he slowly made his way in that direction. Then he saw her, low in a thick mass of ferns and leaves and—hell, yes—he ran the last few yards, practically throwing himself into her.

Her arms wrapped around him and her warm breath blew in hard bursts against his neck. Pulling her onto his lap, he rocked for a few minutes, just holding her and not giving a damn where they were or how they were going to get out. He'd found her.

"They're on my backtrail," she said when the emotional release had run its course. "I hear them shout every once in a while, at a distance."

"We'll move. I just...I just need to hold you a few more seconds."

"I lost you," she said. "I didn't know if you were...I didn't know if you'd be coming, so I had to move."

"My battery pack got wet. It must have been cracked or something, because it shorted on me." There was a *crack* and he lay flat, pulling Carmen with him. "We need to move, babe. I should probably tell you I'm out of ammo, too. I managed to retrieve a couple of weapons from DBs. One guy's was also low on ammo and the other moron had overheated his and melted the fucker."

"So we have a .22 with seven shots. Wonderful."

"Just means we do a lot more running and hiding than fighting. And it's time to run, on my go..."

Rossi stood and stretched his back, taking a few deep breaths. *I see Gallagher. He's on his feet, coming this way.*

It was the miracle he'd been looking for. Almost. But on the heels of that news came Charlotte's report. The guerillas were mobilized, pissed and had a pretty good idea of where their prey had gone to ground. Worse still, Le Roux had called in outlying men to form a new outer perimeter. Finding a place for the helo to rendezvous with Gallagher and Carmen was going to be a logistical nightmare.

Scratch that. It was going to be impossible.

He knocked on the bedroom door and opened it, surprised to see Isabelle Arceneau sitting on the side of the bed, fully awake. "There's stuff going on. I need you to come out here in case we have to move fast."

She didn't hesitate, grabbing her water and following him into the main room. "Is there anything I can do to help? Relay information or...watch a screen or something?"

"Just sit tight. And if we move, grab that black bag right there and stay on my heels."

She nodded and sat quietly in a chair. He knew he should speak to her—reassure her or comfort her, something—but he didn't have it in him. He needed to concentrate on the critical moments ahead.

One mistake could cost lives and he didn't intend for them to be his people.

They ran, dodging from cover to cover but mostly going for distance, then another *crack*. Gallagher hit Carmen in the back and they went down together, so he got yet another face full of damp dirt and plant decomp. It was starting to really piss him off, but the asshole's aim was definitely improving.

"Give me that," he said, reaching for her .22.

"He's out of range, so there's—"

"Give me the goddamn gun." Time for that fucker to eat his share of jungle floor.

He checked the safety, then braced his left shoulder against a tree, waiting.

There.

The fucker was grinning, knowing he was out of range and he took his time raising his own weapon. Came closer. Cocky.

Closer still.

Gallagher raised the .22, found his target.

The target laughed.

Leaning back against the tree, Gallagher pressed the butt of his left hand against the slide. Pulled the trigger with his right hand, restricting the slide's kick with his left, forcing added velocity.

The target stopped laughing and crumpled to the ground.

"Neat trick," Carmen said.

"He was pissing me off. Give me your comm for a few minutes."

She passed it over and then started rebraiding her hair. He paused in settling the earpiece. It was shorter—her hair—and it looked like it had been hacked pretty badly. A story for another day, God willing.

"Hey, Rossi," he said into the mic.

"Holy shit, it's good to hear your voice."

"Likewise, dude, but we need a plan. Yesterday. Between us we have three knives, a flash bang and six .22 shots."

"We're working on it," Rossi told him, his voice brittle with stress. "They've set up an outer perimeter and mounted an organized search pattern, bulk of it coming in from the west. They have an idea where you are and it's a foot race."

"Get O'Brien on."

"Hold on, he's en route."

"I'm here," O'Brien said when he was on comm.

"Dude, you ready to kick it old school?" Gallagher asked him.

It took a few seconds for his brain to catch up. "Jesus, G. Are you shittin' me?"

"What's going on?" Rossi demanded.

"G's carrying a rapid extraction harness. All he needs is a hook. But that's a solo rig."

"I know that," Gallagher said.

Rossi took a moment to swear in two languages, and then he got down to business. "Charlotte, pull up topo and aerial. Tell Tony to find a place where we can do this thing."

"With minimal canopy," O'Brien added. "This is gonna suck for her, big time."

"I'll have Charlotte monitoring the feed," Rossi said. "The provisional government's gonna be pissed we poked the tiger, so we'll evac straight to Gabon. Charlotte will ID the best hospital and have the medical staff there on standby, giving them real time status updates."

Gallagher heard a click as Tony Casavetti joined the conversation from Texas. "How far is Olivera good for?"

"The situation's getting hot, so we'll be going hard. The closer to our current position, the better."

"Half-ass clearing eight-tenths of one mile south-southeast of your position. Light canopy cover."

"I don't have a hook, man," O'Brien said. "I'm going to have to catch it with the skid and Donovan's going to have to get her in."

They talked time, distances and logistics for a few minutes, and then Gallagher was left with nothing but selling Carmen on the plan.

"Come up with something?" she asked when it was obvious the conversation was over.

"Just under a mile from here, there's a clearing. Not enough to land a helo, but enough of a break in the canopy to extract by air."

"What? Like dropping a ladder, or a rescue basket? That helicopter stands still more than a few seconds, those assholes will fill it full of holes."

"It's not going to stand still. Hell, it's barely going to slow down."

He wasn't surprised when she gave him the skeptical raised eyebrow look. It wasn't exactly standard operating procedure.

"It's a harness system," he explained. "There's a ring, and when you pull it, the canisters fire and it's going to send up two balloons. There's a thin cable between them. Since we don't have a C-130, the helo's going to hook the cable with a skid and you'll be flying until they can get you inside. It ain't fun. It'll fuck you up, maybe in a bad way, but it shouldn't kill you."

"That's comforting."

"Down here you *will* die. Less comforting."

"How long until it comes back for a second pass?" He didn't answer, and then she got it. "There's only one harness."

"Getting you out of here is priority one. Alone, I can be invisible."

"I can be invisible, too, you jerk. Most of the time that's my *job*."

"Jungle combat's different, babe."

"Don't babe me. I am *sick* of your condescending, sexist bullshit, and—"

"There's nothing sexist about it. We all have strengths and weaknesses and *your* biggest weakness is your inability to be honest about yours." She opened her mouth, but he bulldozed over her. "I'm in charge of this op and your presence is detrimental to my safety, so I am *ordering* you onto that helo."

A resounding *fuck you* sat on the tip of her tongue, but she didn't spit it at him.

It was all there on his face. In his eyes. Everything he felt for her. His desperate determination to get her out alive. His willingness to do whatever it took—even dying—to make that happen.

His fear for her.

His love.

"You promise me," she said in a low voice, "that if I go, you *will* get out of here alive."

"If I know you're safe, I can do anything, babe. Nothing could keep me from getting back to you."

"You're not bulletproof."

"No, but this is what I'm trained for. Alone, I have a chance." He cupped her cheek in his hand and ran his thumb across her bottom lip. "I've been doing this most of my life."

"You still haven't promised," she whispered, even though she knew it was one he couldn't give. Theirs was a world with no promises.

"I promise you if you get on that chopper, I'll have a fighting chance, and that's all I've ever needed."

That was as close as she was going to get.

He tipped her chin up so she looked him in the eye. "No matter what, you get your ass on that bird."

Carmen nodded once. She would, because that was the only way to save him.

"Let's get the harness on you and then do some stretching. You're about to run the hardest mile of your life, babe."

Rossi ripped his headset off and replaced it with a portable comm unit. It was time to move.

"Isabelle, we're leaving. Make sure your head is covered and try to arrange your *kanga*—your robe thing—to hide your hands."

She obeyed without hesitation while he used the Flash Drive of Doom, as Charlotte called it, to fry each of the computers. Then he made a quick sweep of both rooms, making sure they didn't leave anything that wasn't expendable.

Most of the gear that Gallagher hadn't taken was on the helicopter, so it didn't take long. After making sure his disguise padding was in place, he grabbed the small camera he'd carry as part of their cover.

"Closing up shop," he told Charlotte, so she could let the others know they were done at the Hotel Jardin. "Isabelle, let's go."

"Where are we going?" she asked as he gave her the once over. She'd hidden her hands and the bag well enough with the draped fabric, and her head and face were covered. Hopefully, in the early dawn hours, she wouldn't stand out a blonde, white girl.

"Airport." He grabbed the black bag by the door and slung it over his shoulder. "Now listen to me. We're going to take our time and look relaxed. I'll be talking to you about...whatever.

I've been seen talking to a lot of people for this fake documentary, so we shouldn't attract attention. When we get to the airport, you just do what I say."

He couldn't give her any more direction than that because things were going to get very fluid at that point.

Though he hated the idea of being on the move while things were going down, it was time to get the hell out of Matunisia. As soon as he found the right aircraft to *borrow*, he and Isabelle Arceneau were heading for Gabon.

All he could do was pray he'd be reunited with his team there.

As their pace steadily ate up the distance, Carmen almost convinced herself it was a good plan. Gallagher was the real deal, and he *did* stand a fighting chance with her out of the way. Alone, he could do what he needed to do.

"We're almost there," he called to her, and he didn't even sound winded. "You've got the plan?"

"Yes." She didn't like it, but she got it.

"Just a few more—"

He grunted and she turned her head enough to see him fall in her peripheral vision. She slowed, but he was on his knees, pushing himself to his feet, half-crawling toward her.

"Go." His lips formed the word and her heart broke.

Then he was hit again. And this time he didn't get back up.

No matter what, you get your ass on that bird.

Time seemed to slow to a crawl, and Carmen realized that would be the last time she saw Gallagher. *Ever.* His fighting chance was gone and he was as good as dead.

Assuming he was even still alive.

She spent about five seconds considering the rest of her life without Gallagher in it before she turned, fired three shots into the woods and ran back to him.

He was alive.

Conscious of the critical time slipping away, Carmen dropped the Ruger into her pocket, then crouched and hauled Gallagher across her shoulders in a fireman's carry. Her leg muscles trembled and resisted, but she managed to stand.

Thanking God for every punishing workout she'd ever forced herself to suffer through, she managed to start moving again.

A bullet whizzed past them, thunking into a tree, but Carmen just kept putting one foot in front of the other. They'd make it or they wouldn't, but she wasn't going without him.

"Approaching clearing," she yelled into Gallagher's mic, purposely not giving his status. This was their only shot, and she didn't want them aborting for any reason. "We're under fire."

"Affirmative."

Pain seared across her left side, stealing her breath. She stumbled and Gallagher's weight gave her momentum. They crashed to the ground and he rolled away.

Their numbers were about up, and the adrenaline kicked in in a big way. She scrambled to Gallagher and hoisted him again. There was no time for return fire. No time to wonder if she could do it or not. She just went.

Carmen broke into the clearing. Her breath came in ragged gasps and the pain in her side was excruciating. Her shoulders and legs were screaming and she could almost feel her spine compressing.

She reached the center of the clearing and collapsed.

Gallagher rolled, still unconscious. He was bleeding from a couple of places, but she didn't have time to administer first aid at the moment.

Remembering his instructions, she checked the clips on her harness, then reached behind her back and pulled the pin. There was a popping sound—like a gunshot—and when she looked up she could see the cord making an inverted triangle from her back up to the two balloons.

Carmen dragged Gallagher upright, looking for some way— *any* way—to clip him to her vest. They both had carabiners and she hooked them together. It wasn't enough. There wasn't—

A low, rapid *whoop whoop.*

She grabbed at him, hooking her arms under his and getting a leg under his crotch. Then her entire body jerked— *snapped*—and then she was hurtling through the air.

"Fuck!" She heard O'Brien shout through the disc in Gallagher's ear, and felt the dip as the helo reacted to the excess weight.

Gallagher was slipping. She clawed at the back of his vest, feeling the *pop pop* of agony as her fingernails gave way. She got one leg between his, trying to brace him.

The wind grabbed at her, blinding her and trying to rip Gallagher away. Branches and leaves scored her body like razor blades. Something smacked her hip hard and he slipped again.

Her shoulder tore, muscle ripping away from bone and cartilage. She screamed, searing her vocal cords and allowing the wind into her lungs. Her other fingers found purchase in his vest and she held him, his weight grinding her bones.

Then the wind tried to take him again, and she fought, squeezing him with her legs. It was all she had left.

"Carmen!"

Still she screamed, clinging desperately to him.

"He's in!" A man was shouting at her. "You're both in. You can let him go now, Carmen. *Please* let him go."

The man was untangling her legs, then peeling her throbbing fingers away from Gallagher's vest.

"You're safe now," the man said. It was Jack Donovan, and he was still yelling—she could barely hear him over her own ragged sobs. "We're on our way to a hospital. You hang on."

She wanted to ask if Gallagher was alive, but she couldn't breathe—couldn't talk.

Then the first muscle spasm hit and she screamed again. And kept screaming until the world went blessedly dark.

Alex Rossi was on his knees, the hospital chapel's plain, nondenominational cross looming over him. Despite a Catholic boyhood, he wasn't a praying man. And he wasn't exactly praying then. He was just...waiting. Bargaining. Seeking solace. Hell, he didn't know *what* he was doing.

He didn't need a debriefing. Both guys on the helo were wired for sight and sound, and he'd watched the recorded feed after Gallagher and Carmen were rushed beyond swinging doors he couldn't bully his way through.

He'd watched the skid catch the line in a textbook maneuver from O'Brien's view, and then watched it all go to shit from Donovan's.

As Donovan—clipped to a safety line—had stepped out onto the skid and worked his ass off getting enough cable to feed into an improvised pulley, Rossi had witnessed Carmen's fight for Gallagher's life. He'd seen her pain and he'd heard it. Her screams...

O'Brien had cut Gallagher's microphone, but not before her screams reverberated through their earpieces and his speakers—an agonized, inhuman cry that would haunt each of them for a very long time.

Alex ached for Grace and Danny. He wanted to see them. Needed desperately to hold them until his heart stopped hurting.

Donovan walked up and knelt beside him. "Doc's looking for you."

He sounded too solemn and Alex's fists clenched even tighter. It was time to suck it up. Be a man. Do what he had to do.

His breath hiccupped in his chest.

"Gallagher's still holding his own in surgery," Donovan went on. "But Carmen... You've got the medical power of attorney, so the doctor... It's time to make a decision, boss."

Chapter Fifteen

Gallagher seemed to swim through the murky haze forever before he finally broke the surface. The light was blinding, and there was a lot of beeping and hissing and squeaking of rubber-soled shoes.

Hospital. "Carmen."

Nobody responded, and he thought maybe he hadn't said it out loud. "Where's Carmen?"

His voice was croaky and his mouth was desert-dry, but at least there weren't any big tubes shoved into his sinus cavities. Just a nasal cannula stuck in his nostrils. At least that's what the nurses called it the last time he got shot.

A nurse hovered over him. "Mr. McLaine, you're awake. How do you feel?"

Since that was about the stupidest fucking question he'd ever been asked, he ignored it. "Carmen Olivera. Is she here?"

The nurse's brow furrowed in pseudo-maternal concern. "Let's talk about your pain. On a scale of one to ten?"

Eleven. "Where. The fuck. Is Carmen?"

The nurse slipped away, replaced by a doctor who probably looked intimidating to normal people. "Mr. McLaine, we need to focus on *you* right now. Tell me about your pain."

Gallagher managed to lift his head off the pillow. "We'll be talking about *your* pain if I don't get...some..."

He slipped back into the haze, cursing intravenous morphine.

Jack stood in the small airline terminal, assigned to turn Isabelle over to the reasonably capable-looking federal agents waiting by the doors. They wanted her back in the States ASAP, safe and under wraps.

He was all for her being safe, but now that the time had come to let her go, he didn't know what to say to her.

"I wish I could stay longer," she said, seeming no more eager to head toward the door than he was to send her. "Your friends risked their lives for me and I didn't even get to meet them."

Thinking about Gallagher and Carmen made his gut ache. "Now's not a good time."

"I should say thank you, at least. They helped save me from..." He watched her inhale slowly through her nose, pushing the horror back. "You all saved me."

"You should change your name," he told her. "Maybe take your mother's maiden name. We can help you change your paperwork and find a good therapist. You can make a new life for yourself—whoever you want to be."

"I'm not going to hide from this. I'm going to fight for my father."

"Your father's going to prison. He helped hurt and kill a lot of people, Isabelle."

Her fingers curled into fists as she shook her head. "To save me! He went to Matunisia to *help* those people, and the only reason he got involved with Le Roux was to save my life."

"Everybody knows that, and he'll get some kind of leniency, but the victims have loved ones, too."

"I can't let his life be ruined without a fight. And I'm going to fight for the people you had to leave behind, too. I'm going to shine a spotlight on Le Roux that's so bright the world can't ignore it anymore."

"No." Just the thought of Isabelle being further involved, even from a distance, with the horror show in Matunisia turned his stomach. "You're young, Isabelle. You can still put this all behind you."

"I'm not going to put it behind me, Jack. I'm going to splash this episode of my life on the front pages and tell anybody who'll listen and do whatever I have to do to get to those who won't." The ring of conviction in her voice made him feel old and jaded. "Somebody has to help those people. Why not me?"

Why not somebody he hadn't come to care about quite so damn much? "It's too dangerous."

"So was rescuing me, but you did it anyway. Because somebody had to."

"If you give Le Roux a headache and he gets his hands on you again, I won't be able to ask the Group to go after you. Not if you knowingly put yourself at risk."

"I know. And I only have a few more minutes. I don't want to spend it arguing with you." She gave him a shaky smile and the fight went out of him.

Jack pulled her into his arms, telling himself it was okay to hold her because she was about to get on a plane and he'd probably never see her again.

"I don't want to argue, either," he said into her hair. "I just don't want to imagine you waging a one-woman war against a terrorist. I want to picture you finding a good job, finding a nice...man to marry. Having a family."

With the way her cheek pressed against his chest, he wondered if she could hear his heart thumping.

Her hands slid up his back, coming to rest just below his shoulder blades. "You make it sound like I'm never going to see you again."

"You probably won't."

Her fingers curled against his back. "Why not? I...I want to see you, Jack."

No, she was just afraid of facing the near, uncertain future without her so-called Obi-Wan. "My job was to get you out. I've done that, and now I'll move on to the next job."

"I know you care about me. I can feel it when you hold me, and I see it on your face."

He'd hurt her before for her own good. He could do it again. "It's not real, Isabelle. I was the first guy in a very long time who was nice to you—gentle when I touched you. You've attached yourself to me because I was your rescuer, but it's not real."

Jack felt her surrender. The tension went out of her with a shaky breath and she started to pull away. He resisted letting her go for one short, selfish moment, then dropped his arms.

"It's time for me to go," she whispered, and he used his thumb to wipe away the tear that escaped her eye.

"Isabelle, I..."

"You have a good life, Jack Donovan," she said, and then she spun to walk away.

He grabbed her elbow and she stopped, but didn't turn back. "Isabelle, if you ever need me, you call. Day or night. No matter what I'm doing or where you are, I'll be there."

"I needed you now," she said, and then she walked away—out through the double doors to the plane waiting to take her home.

Jack Donovan let her go, the mistake burning his eyes and squeezing his throat.

The next time he surfaced, Gallagher toed the line. He talked about his pain—a four—and answered every other question asked of him.

He even kept a lid on his temper when they said he wouldn't be getting out of bed anytime soon because of the bullet he'd taken to the thigh, the back of which wasn't protected by the chaps. It had missed the femoral, but it had torn up the muscle and nicked the bone, and he'd lost a lot of blood. He'd also taken one in the back, just below the vest, but it wasn't deep or especially problematic. His body was also a mass of bruises and cuts thanks to his warp speed exit through the treetops.

He just nodded along and gave them his best game face. But all the while he was thinking about Carmen. Why wouldn't they at least tell him if she was alive? He watched enough TV to know they'd withhold bad news from a patient *for his own good.*

The worst case scenario—she was dead in the jungle. He couldn't remember their last minutes on the ground, but there was no other way to explain how he'd come to be the one extracted.

He kept his voice deliberately calm. "Could somebody please tell me if Carmen Olivera is here?"

The doctor barely paused on his way out the door. "We don't give patient information to anybody but immediate family and those with medical power of attorney."

"Can you tell Alex Rossi to get his ass in here?"

"I'm not sure where he is at the moment, and you're

becoming agitated. I'm going to restrict your visitors until you calm down." And then the asshole was gone.

When Gallagher's nurse was finished her poking and prodding, he smiled at her. "Can you get a message to Alex Rossi for me?"

"Yes. Your friends have commandeered one of the waiting rooms and some cots, so I know I can find him. I don't know if the doctor will let him in, though."

"Here's what I want you to say..."

Rossi was on the phone with Charlotte when a nurse knocked and poked her head in the door. "Mr. Rossi?"

"Call you back, Charlotte." He snapped the phone closed, dread chewing up his stomach lining. "Come in."

She did, closing the door behind her. "I'm Molly, Mr. McLaine's day nurse."

"He didn't hurt anybody, did he?" They'd managed to put off giving Gallagher the news for several days, thanks to the drugs, but he was being weaned off. They were running out of time.

"No...well, not yet, anyway. But I'm supposed to ask you, when you had to rescue your son from Contadino's men, who went back for your wife?"

Gallagher watched the minutes tick away on the ugly industrial clock. Only six passed.

"Straight up, Rossi," he said, when his boss had closed the door behind him. "Eleven fucking years I've had your back, and you just fucking abandon me here, telling me nothing?"

"When a doctor tells me something's in the best medical interests of my guy, I listen."

"That's bullshit, and you know it. You don't have the balls to come and talk to me like a man."

Rossi had his laptop and he set it up on the rolling bedside cart. "She's still in ICU."

Tension not even the morphine had touched fell away. "So she's not dead?"

"Oh Christ." Rossi had been plugging in the power cord, but his head snapped up. "You gotta believe me, man. I thought they'd at least told you she was alive."

Gallagher threw his arms over his eyes to hide the leak they were threatening to spring. "I want to see her."

"See this first."

Gallagher wiped his arm across his eyes and turned his head to face the monitor. He watched the video feed of their extraction up to the actual catching of the wire from the pilot's point of view, which had almost no visibility of the ground. But there was a glimpse.

"Pause it. I know we hadn't reached the clearing yet when I went down."

"Judging by some of your bruising and the blood patterns on her clothes, we think she carried you over her shoulders."

"No fucking way." But he knew it had to be the truth. They hadn't reached the extraction point when he went down, and she was the only person on the ground not trying to kill him. "I can't believe it."

"It gets worse, man."

And it did. But Gallagher forced himself to watch every second Donovan's camera had captured. By God, if she could take it, he could watch it.

Until his dead weight ripped her arm out of its socket and he heard her scream.

168

Rossi got an empty bedpan in front of him, but it didn't matter. His stomach had nothing in it to vomit up, and all he could do was dry heave, the wound in his back making itself known with a vengeance.

When that had passed, he watched the rest of the feed, right up until she finally passed out. Alex closed the laptop and sat in the visitor's chair.

"Her shoulder was a fucking mess, but the surgery helped. Most of her fingernails are gone, and she broke three fingers holding your vest's harness. She has a GSW to her left side, mostly a flesh wound. Judging by the bruising, the harness jarred the hell out of her ribs when it lifted her, but the scans didn't show any breaks."

Gallagher was aware of the tears making tracks down his face, but he was beyond giving a shit. "Why didn't she fucking let me go?"

"Same reason you wouldn't have let her go. If it had been any of us, she couldn't have done it. Not wouldn't have, but *couldn't* have. Only one thing makes you superhuman, man."

Love. "When can I see her? I mean, that's some serious shit, but it's not critical."

Rossi stopped making eye contact and Gallagher got scared again. The man was holding something back—something not good.

Rossi scrubbed his hands over his face. "The doctor told me all this shit about adrenaline and endorphins and stuff. Basically, she pushed her body way beyond its limits and he wasn't sure about her mind's ability to cope with the physical aftermath. I signed off on a short-term medically-induced coma. Just so they could get her physically stabilized first."

Gallagher knew all about the let down. He knew if you got a big enough rush, it was like tying on a bad drunk. You could beat the shit out of yourself and not feel it until the next day when the hangover took over.

"So...when the worst is past, he'll just uninduce her or whatever, right?"

"He did that a few hours ago." Rossi drew in a deep breath. "She hasn't come out of it. She's still nonresponsive."

"Why?"

"They don't know."

"What do you mean they don't fucking know?" He cursed the wounds and wires keeping him from beating the answers he wanted out of Rossi.

"The doctor said on some subconscious level Carmen might not be ready to face her physical trauma. As her body recovers, she may regain consciousness."

May. The word stuck in Gallagher's mind, cutting him off from rational thought and clogging his throat. Carmen *may* wake up.

Or she *may* already be gone and her body didn't know it yet.

He wasn't aware Rossi moved until the man gripped his shoulder. "She's never alone, man. I can promise you that."

Gallagher couldn't get any words past the lump in his throat. All he could do was shake his head while more tears filmed over his eyes. Finally he swallowed past it. "I want to see her."

"They don't want you in the ICU right now."

"I don't give a flying fuck what they want."

"Unfortunately you aren't getting in there unless they let you in. But I'll make sure you're in the loop."

He'd see about that.

"Next time you're with Carmen, you tell her..." He tried clearing his throat, but it didn't help. He just couldn't say all the things he wanted Carmen to know.

Rossi's fingers squeezed, then fell away. "She knows. Now I need to go make a few phone calls. There's shit hitting fans all over the damn place. Anything you need before I go?"

Gallagher closed his eyes and nodded. "Carmen."

And damn if it wasn't Rossi who found him two hours later, army crawling his way down the hallway with his hospital johnny flapping and his ass hanging out in the breeze.

"For Christ's sake, I don't need to see that on an empty stomach," his boss's voice said.

"Then go get a fucking sandwich." The pain meds were wearing off and his body was slick with sweat. "Anybody who gets in my way is dead, plain and simple."

It was a slow and painful process. He put his hands out, then dragged his lower body forward. The sweat kept him from getting floor burn on his hip, but his hands were starting to slide a bit.

"How are you planning to get through the ICU doors?"

Gallagher gritted his teeth and hauled himself forward another two feet. "I'll wait 'til somebody comes out and sneak in unnoticed on my stomach."

"One thing you are not right now, man, is unnoticeable."

Then Rossi's hands were under his armpits. Gallagher must have been weaker than he'd thought because the other man had no problem propping him up against the wall like a rag doll. "I don't even want to know how you unhooked yourself from everything you were hooked to, do I?"

"Lucky for me I'd already charmed the nurse into removing

that fucking catheter or I'd still be crying."

"If I can trust you to sit here for a few minutes without killing anybody or making the candy stripers cry, I'll go find a wheelchair and take you to see her."

It took every drop of testosterone in Gallagher's body not to cry. He nodded, then rested his head against the wall.

Chapter Sixteen

As expected, they met resistance at the entrance to ICU. "Doctor Domoraud doesn't want Mr. McLaine in the ICU. He's shown signs of emotional instability and a potentially volatile personality."

There was no potentially about it, and she was going to see that firsthand if she didn't hit the button and let him in.

Rossi turned his chair so he couldn't glare at the nurse in charge. "His emotional instability is a direct result of not being allowed to see Carmen. Give him five minutes with her and he'll be stable again. More or less."

"I'm sorry, Mr. Rossi. I really am. But Doctor Domoraud has given orders and his authority here in the hospital is absolute."

Rossi didn't say anything right away, so Gallagher started building a scenario in his head, just in case.

If he reached down and set the brake on the chair, he might be able to use his arms to launch himself onto his good leg and then spring forward so he was against the nursing station desk. Hit the button. Then push himself back into the chair and—if it didn't fly out from under him and leave him laid out on the floor with a concussion—release the brake and get to the door before it relocked.

It was a long shot, but he wasn't turning back now. He

started turning his chair back to face the desk.

"Is that right?" Rossi finally said. He pulled out his phone and hit two on the speed dial. "Charlotte, I've got a little problem. Doctor Domoraud is denying Gallagher entrance into the ICU and the nurse claims his authority here is absolute. Could you check on that for me? Thanks."

He snapped the phone closed and looked at Nurse Ratched, who only rolled her eyes and walked away.

"If Charlotte gets me in there," Gallagher said, "I'm going all out on her wedding gift."

"Jesus, don't say wedding. She's already scheduling tux fittings. And Grace gets more emails from her with links to bridesmaid dresses than she does penis enlargement offers."

"She sign you up for that yet?"

They both laughed, but it was half-hearted and short. Both men knew things would get ugly if Bridezilla didn't come through.

The longest five minutes of his life passed before the station phone started ringing, drawing the nurse back. A second later Alex's cell followed suit. The nurse's eyes got wide. Alex chuckled at something his caller said. The nurse started stammering. Alex snapped his phone closed. The nurse hung up her line and hit the button to unlock the ICU doors.

Rossi rolled him in. "Charlotte told me to tell you she's registered at Tiffany's and she knows how much you make a year. But you're fading fast man, and you're sweating. Fifteen minutes, but if you're good about it, I'll bring you back tomorrow."

Damn, she was pale. The room, though empty but for Gallagher and Carmen, was a flurry of activity. Machines pumping. Monitor screens beeping and graphing. The blood pressure machine hissing.

But she was perfectly still, like a bruised and bandaged princess from some fairy tale. He rolled as close to the bed as he could and stretched painfully to kiss her cheek, but she didn't stir. Prince Charming, he wasn't.

He didn't know what to do. He wanted to hold her hand, but they were both bandaged. The parts of her body not covered by a blanket or bandage were bruised or scraped, like his own. But her cheek was unmarred, so he settled for stroking it softly with the back of his knuckles.

"They told me you won't wake up, babe," he said, and even though his voice was barely more than a whisper, it sounded loud in the room. "You...you need to wake up. I promise I won't yell at you for not listening to me."

Well, that sounded stupid, so he was silent for a couple of minutes, just stroking her cheek and staring at her beautiful face.

Then he started talking again. He told her about his parents and his sister in San Diego. How he wanted her to meet them. He wanted to take her walking on the beach at twilight.

The minutes ticked by until he knew Rossi would return any time.

"Please wake up, babe. Rossi showed me the feed, so I know how hard you fought not to leave me behind. So don't leave me behind now."

The door opened and closed, and then he felt Rossi's hand on his shoulder. "It's time to go."

"I love you, Carm." He kissed his fingertips, then touched them to her face.

He took a deep breath, then nodded for Rossi to wheel him

out. O'Brien slipped into the room behind them, ready to take his turn at the vigil.

"I'm sorry, John," Rossi said in a heavy voice. "I was trying to do what they said was the best thing for her."

"I would have done the same thing." It would be easy to blame Rossi—to have somebody to take all his bottled up emotions out on. But he was a good guy and Gallagher wouldn't do that to him.

"Tell me somebody's paying for this," he said as they wheeled back to his room.

The first person Carmen saw when she opened her eyes was Jack Donovan, so she closed them again.

Not fast enough. "Carmen!"

She didn't want to talk to Jack. Or the nurses she heard coming through the door. She wanted Gallagher. *John.*

"She opened her eyes," she heard Jack tell the nurses. "She's awake."

"We'll need you to leave, Mr. Donovan."

"Wait, I need to—"

"Now."

"He made it, Carm," she heard him call before the door whooshed closed.

He made it. She opened her eyes again.

There was poking and prodding, things removed and things added, pinpricks and endless questions. She suffered it all gladly, because at the end—*soon*—she'd see John.

"I want out of this damn chair."

Gallagher was in the waiting room the Group had

commandeered for the duration. He'd taken to wheeling himself around when he couldn't stand the sight of his own four walls anymore—which was often. In the week since his first visit to Carmen, he'd been spending much of his time in her room or here, much to the annoyance of his nurse, who grumbled loudly and often about having to chase him around the hospital with the blood pressure cuff.

Rossi was stretched out on a cot, staring up at the ceiling. "For the thousandth time, you can't have crutches because of the damn bullet hole in your back. And if you're going to keep whining, go back to your room and do it."

"I'm not whining. The faster I get out of this chair, the faster I'm back on the job."

"If you really want back on the job, go read the reports Marge sent over."

Gallagher snorted. "Fat chance. Reading reports is why you make the bigger bucks. What's the status on Le Roux today?"

"The provisional government's not going after him. Loss of life and collateral damage would be astronomical, they say, even with the camp in chaos." Rossi swung his legs to the floor and sat on the edge of the cot. "He's untouchable in that compound, man."

"Fuck that. I'll reach out and touch his ass—with a fifty-cal round. He's not getting away with this."

The door to the waiting room opened and Donovan stepped in. Gallagher could see he'd been running and his stomach dropped. He was supposed to be with Carmen.

"She opened her eyes."

They made him wait for what seemed like forever. Stuck in the damn wheelchair, he couldn't even pace off any of the tension.

So much of his job was about waiting—waiting for the right moment, the right plan, the right shot. But every lesson he'd ever learned in patience had escaped him. He wanted through those doors.

And the nurse at the desk knew it, too. She was watching him like he was a carb whore three feet from a doughnut.

Finally the door opened and the doctor stepped out. "Everything looks good. She's tired, and she has some pain, but we want to keep medications to the minimum she can stand. She's a strong woman."

Gallagher nodded, unable to come up with the right words to express just how much he agreed.

"She's asking for you," the doctor said to him. "I need to spend a little more time with her, do some assessments and such, but I'll give you two minutes with her first. *Two.*"

Carmen was groggy and hurt in more places than even that soap commercial claimed existed, but seeing Gallagher roll into her room made it all worthwhile. He paused at the door and the way he looked at her made her shiver.

"Hey, babe."

She wanted to reach out to him, but the splints on her hand were too heavy to lift, and her other arm was totally immobilized for her shoulder. But she could smile. "Hey, you."

Gallagher rolled his chair up to her bed, and when he reached out and touched her face, tears spilled over onto her cheeks.

"Don't cry, babe." He wiped them away, his touch more gentle than she'd thought possible from him. "If you cry, I'll cry again and I have a reputation to protect, you know."

"You cried for me?"

"There's nothing I wouldn't do for you, Carmen."

It was too much—too intense—and she wasn't strong enough for this yet. "A diet would have been nice."

He laughed and a nurse peeked in to sternly shush him. "Sorry, babe. But if you'd obeyed my orders, my weight wouldn't have mattered."

"When you fell, I realized if I got on that helicopter, I'd never see you again. I wasn't ready to spend the rest of my life without you."

"Does that mean you're ready to spend the rest of it *with* me?"

"I don't know." She saw the brutality of her answer in his eyes, but she wouldn't be anything less than honest with him. "From that moment to now has literally been a blink of the eye for me, John. I need time to process what happened and...how I guess I feel."

"I know, babe." The door opened and his shoulders slumped. "Time's up. Call my room when you're up to another visit. If I'm not there, I'm with Rossi so call his cell. They hid mine."

"Are they going after...him?" No names in front of the nurse. "While there's some turmoil?"

"No. They don't have the balls to take him on."

The frustration she heard in his voice mirrored what Carmen felt. While their primary objective had been met— Isabelle Arceneau was safe and her father spilling his guts— knowing Le Roux was still out there, no doubt holding other loved ones for ransom, was a bitter pill to swallow.

"We'll get him," he said as the nurse dragged his wheelchair toward the door. His tone was easy-going, but there was a look in his eyes that said John Gallagher McLaine wasn't done with Le Roux. Not by a long shot.

Gallagher had been expecting a summons, but the boss waited until the rush of Carmen's improving condition calmed down to call him in for a meeting. He didn't have a good feeling about the next couple of minutes, so he took his time, and Rossi turning off the news when he walked in was definitely a bad sign.

"Sit down," his boss ordered, but he didn't, so they both stood. "I've trusted you with my life. With Grace and Danny's lives. And at some point over the years you've held the lives of each and every Devlin Group agent in your hands."

And nobody had ever been left behind, but he didn't bother pointing that out. He'd known there was an ass-chewing with his name on it waiting.

"Every agent in the field trusts you—not because I do, but because you've earned it. They're conditioned to obey you without question and without hesitation. You broke that trust, John."

"O'Brien did *not* obey me without hesitation. He fucking left her to die."

"You made the call to jeopardize two agents *and* the package for one agent."

"Bullshit!" He stepped forward and got in Rossi's face, though he kept his hands down. "If O'Brien had tossed Donovan a gun and got that truck moving, they could have gotten her out."

"Are you denying your personal feelings for Carmen factored into your decision?"

"Are you denying fucking Donovan's screaming to get

Isabelle out factored into O'Brien's decision? Donovan's feelings for that girl overrode their willingness to go after Carmen."

Rossi's face was turning red, and anybody else would have backed down. Gallagher poked a finger at his chest. "I would have made the same call if you were pinned down, or O'Brien, or anybody. And you know it."

"You look me in the eye and tell me your feelings for Carmen had nothing to do with your call."

"You want me to lie to you?" Gallagher shouted. "You know goddamn well how I feel about Carmen and that I didn't want them to leave her. But that doesn't mean it was the wrong call."

"And that doesn't mean you made it for the right reasons." The fight went out of Rossi and he sank into a chair. "I don't know what I'd do if Grace was still in the field."

Since they weren't going to take their disagreement to a physical level, Gallagher figured he may as well sit, too. And he also knew he was facing the one man he could bare his soul to. "I don't know, all right? I think they could have gotten her out, but I don't know if that's hindsight."

"I wasn't there. You sounded like you were running on emotion, but I can't put myself in your head." He ran his hands through his hair.

"Which one said something?"

"Donovan, but his head's all fucked up over that girl, so I don't know. You were *both* running on emotion, and that's not good."

"I can't promise you I'll lock my feelings in a box on every job. Even though she quit before you got married, you and Grace were partners and lovers at the same time. You've been there. But I *can* promise that, while I'd give my life for Carmen, I'd never make that decision for another agent."

"I hope you're right. Just because the Group is what it is today largely because of you, don't think I won't kick your ass up around your ears if you fuck up again."

Jack Donovan wished he were a drinking man. Or a drug addict. Or maybe suffering from short-term memory loss.

He'd suffer almost anything if it would erase Isabelle Arceneau from his memory.

She was too young for him.

She'd been traumatized.

He should have kissed her. Just once.

Dammit. He grabbed his keys and left his motel room, hell-bent on...something. Anything besides brooding. He was still idling at the exit of the parking lot when his phone buzzed him with a text.

Meet me on the bench at main entrance. G.

At least it was a destination. A distraction.

By the time he found a parking space and walked halfway around the building, Gallagher was already waiting, his wheelchair parked next to the bench. While he was on his feet, the wheelchair was a condition of his being allowed outside until his discharge.

"How you feeling?" he asked, settling on the bench.

"Not bad for somebody who just got his ass handed to him on a plate by Rossi."

"We couldn't wait."

Gallagher held up a hand. "I had to get Carmen out and you had to get Isabelle out. We both had personal objectives fucking up the works, but we all got out and I got no hard feelings."

"I've still got your back. Anytime, anywhere. You know that."

"Good." Gallagher grinned and Donovan knew he was up to something. And it would be something no good. "I'm cleared for discharge as soon as they get the paperwork together, but they're holding Carmen another thirty-six to forty-eight. I'm thinking about taking a little field trip before we fly home."

"Need a chaperone?"

"I can't drive yet, plus I was thinking more like a spotter."

The hair on the back of Donovan's neck tingled. *Hell, yeah.* Better than drugs, alcohol *or* a head injury. "I'm in. Is this a field trip off the reservation?"

Not that it mattered. It was worth Donovan's job if it came to that.

"Let's just say the boss was careful not to read the permission slip before he signed the bottom."

Chapter Seventeen

Neither man had packed a ghillie suit for their Matunisian jaunt, so they'd assembled their own from branches and ferns. Analyzing the photos and the video feeds tech support had collected while hunting for Gallagher and Carmen had offered up a good spot—isolated, easy retreat and with a clear shot to Le Roux's front door.

Granted, it was one-point-two-six miles from the front door, but Rossi had helpfully absconded with his wife's TAC-50 rifle when she left the Group and it had made the trip with them.

With Gallagher nursing a couple of gunshot wounds, running was out, so after landing back in Matunisia, they'd scrounged a couple of dirt bikes, loaded them in the back of a truck they rented and set out.

Now, camouflaged and ready, they waited. And waited.

It was a perfect day. No wind. Humidity and terrain already factored. All they needed was for Le Roux to poke his head out and stand still long enough to get a reading.

Boom.

Gallagher had already mentally run through every possible excuse he could give Carmen for not telling her he was going back into the jungle, and he'd discarded every one of them.

She was going to be pissed. No way around that. But there

was no way she'd have stayed in bed, recuperating and regaining her strength, if she knew he'd be spending the day less than a mile and a half from the compound.

"I don't want to do it this way," Donovan said, breaking the silence in a low voice. "I want to go down there in the middle of the night and rip his heart out with my bare hands while he's sleeping."

"I don't plan on ever coming back to this hellhole, but you and O'Brien can't do it alone. Which you'd have to since I sure as hell couldn't help." But he knew exactly how the other man felt. There wasn't anywhere near enough violence in the impending shot to assuage their anger. "It's this or he keeps breathing. We can't get to him. Especially now, with their paranoia on high."

"I get that. I just want to *hurt* him. To feel him die."

He knew right where that was coming from. "You gonna check on Isabelle Arceneau when we get back to the States?"

Donovan was quiet for a minute, then a negative twitch of his head. "No. The job is done and feds will take care of her now."

"Don't bullshit me, dude."

"No, I'm not going to look her up, G. She's twenty-three. She's spent almost two years being raped and abused by God knows how many of those fucking animals down there."

"Rossi and O'Brien both said she had some grit. She'll get past this. And I hate to bring it up, but don't forget you were wired, man. You two had a connection."

"Of course we had a fucking connection. I was the first guy in two fucking years to not beat her and worse, and I was taking her out of there. Taking advantage of a case of hero worship from a traumatized woman—hell, barely a woman— would make me one sick bastard."

Shannon Stacey

"Or maybe she's a young woman strong enough to survive hell who knows a good man when she sees one."

"Fuck you, G. She's gone. Let it—he's out."

And there the bastard was, coming out of the command building with a couple of his so-called lieutenants right behind him. And then—thank you, God—he stopped, listening to a young guerilla who'd trotted up to him.

Donovan's voice was a constant beside him. Height, distance, wind, drop—a flurry of numbers. Gallagher corrected the TAC-50, subtle, almost microscopic adjustments.

Donovan blew out a breath. "Do it."

Gallagher took the shot.

Le Roux fell in the dirt, a blossom of red over his heart. There was a long moment of stunned disbelief in which nobody moved.

Gallagher watched through his scope—watched the scramble for cover, the lieutenants trying to put pressure on the wound. One felt for a pulse, then dropped, stunned to his knees, shaking his head.

It was done.

Shucking off the ghillie suits, Gallagher and Donovan walked the short distance back to the dirt bikes in silence.

Carmen hated the clock. The incessant tick of the second hand slowed to a crawl when she was alone, but it went into overdrive whenever she had company. Especially if it was Gallagher.

But she hadn't had to worry about the turbo ticking today because the bastard hadn't been to see her.

She'd tried patience and understanding—he was probably holed up with Rossi somewhere, scheming—but that only lasted

186

a couple of hours. Then she'd tried calling him, but his phone was turned off.

Odd, but she didn't get too concerned. If anything was wrong, somebody would have told her. She hoped.

Daytime television in the US sucked, and it was even worse in Gabon. When she grew tired of clicking through the channel loop, she shut it off and picked up one of the books the nurses had left on her bedside table. That held her attention for a whopping forty-five minutes.

When Rossi finally popped in, he just shrugged off her question and said Gallagher was off somewhere with Jack Donovan. She didn't get any further with O'Brien, who claimed no knowledge of their whereabouts. She even called Charlotte, who would only tell her Gallagher had called in personal time and gone off the grid.

She slept for a while, until the nurse woke her to take her blood pressure yet again and warn her lunch would be served soon. Cranky and out of sorts, the nurse's good mood grated on her, no doubt causing the woman's scowl at the blood pressure readings.

"Did you hear the news?" the nurse asked because it seemed to be in a handbook somewhere they should make inane conversation with grumpy, half-asleep patients.

"No." Which should have been obvious because she'd been *sleeping.*

"Le Roux was assassinated," the woman whispered, as if saying the man's name too loud would summon his vengeance-seeking ghost to the room.

Years of experience lying kept Carmen's facial expression mildly interested, but inside she totally fell apart.

That's where he'd been. While she was watching the clock and crappy television, that dumb son of a bitch had gone back into the jungle. Because she'd been hurt.

If they'd made a clean exit, he would have walked away. Let somebody else deal with the bastard eventually.

"Did...do they know who did it?" she asked when it was obvious the nurse was expecting some kind of reaction, like jumping out of bed and doing cartwheels or something ridiculous.

No. No was the answer she was looking for. Anything else meant best case he'd been caught, worst case he was...

She was going to kill him.

"No. Some say the shot was from so far away they didn't even hear it."

So Gallagher had been the one on the trigger. Donovan, his cohort in crime who was also going to get his ass kicked, would have been the spotter.

"They say he just fell over dead with a bullet hole in his heart," the nurse continued, no longer even pretending to care what Carmen's pulse rate was. Probably a good thing.

She wanted to grab the nurse by the throat and shake answers out of her. Was there anything else on the news? Any reports of Americans being arrested or killed? Any unrecognizable bodies lying around out there?

She'd dragged his sorry carcass through the jungle to get him out, and he'd gone back in.

By the time Gallagher strolled in, sixteen hours after his last visit and with a plain brown bag in his hand, Carmen had worked herself into a decent state of pissed off.

"Hey, babe," he said, leaning over to kiss her.

She didn't turn her face away, but she didn't throw a lot of enthusiasm behind it, either. Of course he didn't notice.

"Interesting gossip going around the nurse's station this morning," she said in a tone that he *did* notice.

"I must have missed it. Donovan and I went for a little drive."

"You barely got medical clearance to leave the hospital grounds, so I don't think—"

His face changed, the relaxed guy morphing in the space of a heartbeat into warrior guy. "It's done."

"Did you stop and think what it would have done to me if Rossi came in here and told me you were dead? That after...after *all that*, you went back and let them kill you after all?"

"I couldn't handle him being on the planet, Carmen. He owed us too much, and wanting to collect that debt would have eaten me up."

She was running out of steam. What he'd done was stupid and reckless and if she was stronger she'd have slapped him upside the head, but the decision he'd made was a part of who he was.

"Hey, babe, you're not trying to roll me up in bubble wrap, are you?" he teased as the charming guy slipped back to the surface, and she laughed.

Le Roux was dead. Some other greedy, bloodthirsty monster would no doubt step up and take his place, but if the Matunisian government had either brains or balls, they'd strike now and strike hard.

The most important thing was that the Devlin Group's work there was over.

"You'll be getting sprung soon," Gallagher said, as if he'd read her mind, "and we can all head home. Got any plans for next week?"

"I'm going to hole up in my apartment with my Netflix pile, some baked goods, and too much coffee." Would he invite himself over? Or was he going to head off solo into the sunset?

"How about you take a little detour with me first?"

"Do I look like I'm up for traveling?"

"Come spend a weekend in San Diego with me and—"

"Oh, hell no! I'm not playing meet the parents." Just the idea of it made her want to pull the blanket up over her head.

"Even if I brought you a present?"

The excited jump in her belly made her scowl. She was an adult, for God's sake. He wanted to sleep with her again, so of course he brought her a present. Probably something skimpy and easily removed.

From the paper bag, he pulled a beautifully—and no doubt professionally—wrapped box and set it on her lap.

He had to help her take the ribbons off and he cursed himself the entire time. "I can't believe I was so stupid. I should have thought of your hands."

"Shut up. I've never had pretty ribbons on a present, so don't ruin it for me."

He slit the tape for her, too, and she gingerly peeled back the paper, not wanting to tear it. A plain white box dragged the anticipation out until she felt like a little girl on Christmas morning.

Finally she managed to open the lid and pull out the tissue paper. Inside was a bottle of scented lotion—mandarin.

"They didn't have a big selection at the gift shop," he said, talking too fast as though he was nervous. As if he didn't know he'd just given her the best present of her life. "So I made O'Brien drive me down the street to the...whatever you call it. The smelly lotion place. The girl said lavender was a soothing scent, but you said you don't like flowery shit. Oh, and O'Brien and I almost came to blows over whether vanilla's a flower or a fruit. We still don't know."

He didn't seem to notice she hadn't said anything. That she *couldn't* say anything because her throat was clogged with emotion.

"They had grapefruit, but she said that was energizing, which would suck when you're stuck in the hospital. And they had peach, but horny's probably not so good, either. So we kept trying them out until we both smelled like a fucking fruit salad. I picked mandarin because the woman said it promotes serenity and tranquility, so—"

"I love you."

"—I bought that one. What?"

"I love you." And then, to her horror, a tear trickled down her cheek.

She'd hadn't said those words since her mother died, and the emotional rush of putting them out there seemed to break through the dam and more tears followed.

"Oh shit. Carmen?" He grabbed four or five tissues from the box on her bedside table and shoved them at her. "Please don't cry, babe. Shit. I'm sorry."

Unfortunately, his utter helplessness in the face of her tears made her laugh, which killed her bruised ribs, limiting her to a weird wheezing, hiccupping sound.

"Jeez, Carm." He screwed the lid off the lotion and waved it under her nose. "Here, be serene. Tranquil, whatever."

It took the nurse and the threat of Gallagher being expelled from her room to calm things down.

"Are you serious?" He recapped the lotion and set it down so he could touch her. "Because I've risked my life for you, and gone through hell for you. I've taken *bullets* for you, and now I buy you some fruity cream shit and you love me?"

"Yes, I love you because you bought me fruity cream shit. And yes, I'm serious."

She'd never been more sure of anything, even if she couldn't explain it. Of all the things in the world he could have given her, Gallagher had guessed she missed her lotions. *And* he'd remembered she didn't like flower-based scents. What kind of man did that?

The kind of man she could trust her heart to. A man who would treasure the love she gave him.

"I know I told you this once already," Gallagher said, "but you were in a coma at the time, so...I love you, Carmen."

"I've never baked a ham."

"All I want is to come home to you—to wake up next to you every morning. I can live without baked ham, without children, without whatever you don't want to have, but I can't live without you...darling."

She laughed again, pressing her arm across her torso when her ribs protested. "*Darling?*"

"Too much? How 'bout sweetie? Honeybuns?"

Overcome by a case of the giggles, she could only shake her head.

Then he stroked the side of her face, his gaze growing intense and serious. "I can't live without you, babe. You're it for me."

She kissed the palm of his hand. "You're it for me, too. Go tell Rossi to sign me out of here so we can go home."

Epilogue

She'd been right. Gallagher's family home was surrounded by a white picket fence. She'd been wrong about the dog, though. It was a black lab, not a retriever, and it launched itself at Gallagher the second they stepped through the gate.

Stiff as he was, he managed to give the dog a good tussle before two women she assumed were his mother and sister managed to get through the doorway at the same time.

"Johnny!" In stereo.

The girl got there first, running and yelling, "Houston, am I cleared for landing?"

"Negative, flight."

She pulled up short and wrapped her brother in a delicate hug, letting him shield his wounds, and then his mother did the same.

Right behind them was a distinguished, older version of Gallagher. Not bad, Carmen thought, if that's what she had to look forward to.

"You must be Carmen!" Gallagher's mother found her way around the sling and bandages and wrapped her in a maternal hug that smelled like citrus and mint. "It looks like you both found some trouble. Are you healing up okay?"

"Yes, ma'am."

"Johnny, you should have told us you were bringing Carmen home."

"She's a surprise."

"I don't want to put you out, Mrs. McLaine. I'll stay at a motel and—"

"No you won't. Call me Paulie, and we have a guest room. I just wish I'd made a nicer dinner. I always just bake a ham on Sundays."

Carmen laughed. "Did he tell you to say that?"

"She's afraid now that we'll be living in sin, I'll expect her to bake me a ham every Sunday."

"Don't be silly," Paulie said. "You only do that when you're married."

Carmen was introduced to Gallagher's sixteen-year-old sister, Stephanie, and his father, Joe, before they went into the house. Sheba, the lab, ran in crazy circles around their feet, unable to contain her joy.

The house was clean, cozy and comfortable—the kind of home where you could kick back and put your feet up. Gallagher and Joe did exactly that in front of the television, leaving Carmen to assume that because she had breasts, she should follow Paulie and Stephanie into the kitchen.

"So, Johnny tells me you're one of the best agents he's ever worked with," Paulie remarked as she distributed salad fixings to be sliced and diced. Carmen was given light duty—shredding lettuce—either because of her injuries or her status as guest.

The praise definitely made her feel warm and fuzzy, but she wasn't comfortable in the spotlight. "He tells you about his work?"

"In very broad strokes, yes. He takes every precaution to keep us removed from it, but he likes us to be careful—to be aware of anything out of the ordinary and to know who to call if there's a problem."

"We worry about him when he's gone," Stephanie added, "but he always comes home."

Carmen smiled when the girl rapped her knuckles on the butcher block counter. "He's the best at what he does."

"And surrounded by the best." Paulie winked and dumped diced tomatoes into the bowl. "I made a peach cobbler for dessert, Carmen. Do you like peaches?"

Two hours later, Carmen curled up next to Gallagher on the front porch swing and rested her head on his shoulder. "I am *so* full."

"Mom knows how to set a spread."

"I know why you brought me here and had your mother stuff me with peach cobbler."

"Ah, the diabolical cobbler plan. It was supposed to be a little more covert."

"You want me to be so enamored with your family I'll be dying for my own and start popping out Gallagher Juniors every fourteen months."

He laughed at her, loudly enough to make Sheba sit up and bark. "Sorry. I'm just trying to picture you chasing six little versions of me around the house."

"I'm never having sex again." Even now her biological clock didn't offer up even a half-hearted tick.

"Listen, babe. I brought you here because I wanted my family to meet you. Because they're a big part of my life and I just wanted you to come here with me."

"I'm glad you did. Really. I like your family a lot."

"I'll be honest, though. I'm a pretty old-fashioned guy and

195

eventually I'm going to want to call you my wife. I'll behave as long as I can, but eventually I'm going to propose."

She lifted her head from his shoulder so she could see his face. He looked back at her, his gaze steady and warm and loving. This guy wouldn't ever quit on her. "I was thinking on the way home we could make a quick stop in Vegas?"

A squeal from beyond the window behind them proved Gallagher wasn't the only McLaine with the stealth gene, and they both laughed.

"We've got less than a minute before my mom comes flying out that door, so do you really mean that?"

She did. "Yes. I want to marry you. And I don't want all that crap Charlotte's doing, so let's just do it."

He kissed her until his family couldn't contain themselves anymore and spilled out the door. Many hugs, tears and smiles later, Gallagher put his arm around Carmen and whispered in her ear.

"What the hell are we going to call you? Mrs. Gallagher or Mrs. McLaine?"

She turned her face for a kiss, whispering against his lips, "You can call me babe."

About the Author

Shannon Stacey married her Prince Charming in 1993 and is the proud mother of a future Nobel Prize for Science-winning bookworm and an adrenaline junkie with a flair for drama. She lives in New England, where her two favorite activities are trying to stay warm and writing stories of happily ever after.

You can contact Shannon through her website: www.shannonstacey.com

He makes the rules. She breaks them.
This battle of wills just crossed the line...to deadly.

I'd Rather Be in Paris
© *2009 Misty Evans*
Super Agent Series, Book 2

Elite CIA operative Zara Morgan has a reputation as a loose cannon with a penchant for breaking the rules. Now she's got a chance to prove she can be a competent field officer, but the test doesn't end there. She's been paired with sexy covert ops team leader Lawson Vaughn, a man who lives and breathes protocol.

Methodical is Lawson's middle name. He specializes in high-risk search and rescue, not missions that involve tracking down terrorists. Especially while trying to keep the lid on a partner who has a problem with authority and skates by on wits and bravado.

Even before they get on the plane for Paris they're under each other's skin...and fighting a scorching sexual attraction. Drawn into an unauthorized game of vengeance, Lawson is forced to dance a tightrope in order to protect his partner from their quarry—a terrorist who's about to unleash a biological nightmare on the Muslim world. And Zara is the first target.

With her life, and that of millions of innocent people, on the line, Lawson must become the one thing he despises. A renegade.

Warning: Either you're in or you're out. There's no playing it safe anymore.

Available now in ebook and print from Samhain Publishing.

GREAT cheap fun

Discover eBooks!

THE FASTEST WAY TO GET THE HOTTEST NAMES

Get your favorite authors on your favorite reader, long before they're
out in print! Ebooks from Samhain go wherever you go, and work with
whatever you carry—Palm, PDF, Mobi, and more.

Samhain
Publishing, Ltd

LaVergne, TN USA
01 June 2010
184584LV00004B/2/P